Useless Dog

Illustrated by
Jim Marsh

Useless Dog

Billy C. Clark

Edited by
James M. Gifford
Chuck D. Charles
Patricia A. Hall

The Jesse Stuart Foundation
Ashland, Kentucky
1996

Useless Dog
Copyright © 1961 by Billy C. Clark
Copyright © 1989 by Billy C. Clark

Library of Congress Cataloging-in-Publication Data

Clark, Billy C. (Billy Curtis)
    Useless dog / by Billy C. Clark ; edited by James M. Gifford,
Chuck D. Charles, Patricia A. Hall ; illustrated by Jim Marsh.
        p.   cm.
    Summary: Thirteen-year-old Caleb trades a small pig for an old,
ugly, crippled dog that nobody wants and he and the dog soon become
inseparable friends.
    ISBN 0-945084-57-9 (alk. paper)
    [1. Dogs--Fiction. 2. Mountain life--Fiction. 3. Friendship--Fiction.]
I. Gifford, James M.   II. Charles, Chuck D.   III. Hall, Patricia A., 1945- .
IV. Marsh, Jim, 1933- ill.   V. Title.
PZ7. C535Us   1996
[Fic]--dc20   96-14489
                                                                        CIP
                                                                        AC

Published by:
The Jesse Stuart Foundation
P.O. Box 391
Ashland, KY 41114
1996

*To my wife Ruth, my son Billy,
my daughter Melissa, and
my three grandchildren Benjamin,
Timothy, and Jodie Elisabeth.*

Chapter One

I don't rightly know where the big, ugly dog came from in the beginning. I do know that when I found him he was a dog that nobody wanted. Not even me...that is at first.

It was Ma that named him. She named him on the spur of the moment. She just placed her hands on her hips and stared right down into his sad eyes and said to him: "He is nothing but an old outcast. Worst of the lot."

He had a heap of fixing up to do to change Ma's opinion. And inside his ugly old head he found a way to do it. Fact is, he swelled Ma's heart until it was as big as a mountain. Even so, he carried the name Outcast with him to the grave.

I was thirteen at the time and fairly itching all over to own my own dog. There had been dogs on the place but they had always belonged to Pa. And a hound-dog just ain't got room in his heart for two masters. He is sure to hunt his very heart out for his master and that is the way it should be. But we had gone two years without a dog. The last one had been a big rangy bluetick that Pa had named Big Joe. Big Joe was old and nearly blind when he fell off a rock cliff while hunting. Pa had buried him there, close to the rocks, where he would have shelter from the weather. He placed a little dogwood cross above his head. It was lonely without a dog. And Pa, still lonely for Big Joe, seemed content to go forever without another dog.

Ma had never put much stock in hound-dogs. She didn't like Big Joe. He had slept under the house in a small pocket of earth he had dug out just under the floor of my room. One summer his fleas managed to make it through the cracks of the floor and into the ticking of my bed. I scratched until I looked like I had been caught in a nettle patch before I told Ma about the fleas. Ma just fussed! She swore then and there that hound-dogs were useless.

I thought: If I was to ever have a dog of my own, Ma must be the first to soften on the idea. So I set about to soften her on my getting one with the patience of doodling up a doodlebug. I calked the cracks in the floor of my room with pine resin until not a whisper of wind could seep through.

"I'd just like to see a flea get through the cracks of that floor now!" I said to her one day.

"So would I," she answered, not bothering to look up from her milk churn, "being as there is no dog on the place and not likely to be one."

I saw it would be a hard fight to win her over.

Spring had seeped in among the hills before I found a way to soften her. Well . . . I can't rightly claim credit for finding the way, I just took advantage of it when it came. I never really knew until that spring that hill varmints could be so smart. Coon, squirrel, groundhog, and rabbits seemed to sense that we had no dog on the place. That spring they stuck their heads out of the edge of the woods and watched us put our seed in the ground. When our backs were turned the coons dug up the tiny corn kernels. Then the groundhogs and rabbits nibbled away at the cabbage sets and left the small stubs to brown under the sun. We replanted and the groundhogs chipped most of the tiny corn shoots that managed to break ground. And the squirrels and coons waited with the patience of Job for ears to come on the stalks that the groundhogs missed.

I took Pa's rifle with me during the daylight hours. Although I was almost as good a shot as Pa, I just couldn't hit a thing that spring. Not that I could have done a lot of good anyway. After a few cracks of the rifle the varmints chose to come at nights. Only one thing stood a chance of stopping them—a hound-dog. Most of the garden was gone before Ma reckoned that the hill varmints were worse than a hound-dog would be on the place.

But Ma's softening was not all I needed. Hound-dogs cost money, something that was scarce among the valley people, living on poor land. Pa managed to scratch out a living and that was about all. All that he owned he had earned. This was as it should be, he figured. So when I wanted to own a hound-dog, he struck a bargain with me.

Pa had traded four saddleback hogs for an old cow that he had named Muley because she had been born without a sign of horns. He had walked her home behind his wagon. The five mile walk from the small town of Catlettsburg had made her furious. She won Ma's heart right off with the amount of rich milk she gave. But to me she was just plain ornery. She seemed to enjoy aggravating me. She was a pure rogue, despite what Ma said in her favor. If I could have woven together the miles I chased that cow like a man braids a bullwhip, I could have stood on a knoll and cracked the sky with the tip of it.

But it turned out that this old rogue would furnish me with the way to get a hound-dog. She was going to drop a calf in the spring. If I tended that cow, herding her over the mountains to bring her in for milking, I could have her calf come spring to bargain for a hound dog at the stock sales.

I made it through the long winter. But when spring came the old rogue, tried to slip away from me on top of the mountain, lost her footing and slid halfway down the side, hit a tree and killed the calf before it was born. I could have just sat down under the trees and cried.

"You kept your part of the bargain," Pa said, "and I'll keep my end of it." And he offered me the biggest of his shoats to bargain with at the sales.

"There's a heap of difference between a calf and a shoat," I said, shaming myself right off and showing a lack of appreciation for what Pa was doing for me. Pa had been a fighter all his life, and he had no use for a quitter.

"I guess I just misjudged how bad you wanted a dog," he said.

I was too ashamed to look Pa in the eyes. But I said: "I'm mighty grateful for the shoat, Pa."

"You'll just have to make up the difference," Pa said. "Maybe you can bargain for a younger dog; one that you will have to train. That will be for the best anyway. The two of you can learn the hills together. Well, the stock sales are a month away. That will give you enough time to think about the sort of dog you want and practice bargaining."

My face still smarted from the shame of showing my ingratitude. To show Pa that I was enough like him to fight the odds, I said: "I'll just take that little saddleback runt of the litter to do my bargaining with."

"The choice is yours," Pa said, ending it then and there. I fairly expected—fairly hoped—that Pa would try to talk me out of the runt. It would be hard enough to bargain with a bigger shoat. I had surely heaped the odds against me this time. I had just talked too much!

Chapter Two

I kept myself busy during the long days that followed. During the lonesome nights, I lay in bed and thought about getting my own hound-dog and the waiting was almost unbearable. The wind made a mournful sound as it crawled down the mountains. Birds chattered under the eaves of the house and now and then an owl hooted from far off in the woods. Crickets made a ringing noise in my ears like tiny bells and branch frogs screeched like the dry handle of a well pump. I thought hard about the sort of dog I wanted. Trying to drive away the loneliness of the night, I thought, too, of choosing the runt shoat. Maybe I wouldn't be able to trade the runt for a hound-dog. Then I thought of traipsing the hills alone and I knew the world around me would be an ugly, lonesome place for a boy without a dog.

I found fault in Pa's land. The bony ridges were shaped like the point of a lay-off plow, high up where the wind played forever among the peaks. Everywhere the land was rough. Down from the peaks it lay like the knotted fist of an old man, heavy with warts and wrinkles. On one of the levelest knuckles, Pa had built our house many years ago when he had came into the Kentucky country. And old Bossin, our gray-slated work mule, had spiraled around it pulling a plow until the land became too steep for him to stand. There just wasn't enough level land. The red clay earth glistened under the sun like a snail's path across a rock, and it sprouted ribbly corn. But Pa just stuck out his chest and beat the poorness of the earth by planting twice as much to make up the difference in the yield. It had been the best he could afford to buy when he had settled here. He seemed to enjoy fighting the land, looking far ahead, then making his dream into truth. He never envied our neighbor Tom Turner's land, although Tom Turner owned the best strip of land in the country. It seemed to stretch out from the bottom of Pa's mountain just like bread dough, kneaded by a summer wind to a man's liking. It was rich and pretty. Tom Turner wasn't very neighborly. He kept his land posted, and did not allow anyone to walk across it. He raised prize foxhounds and sheep. A strong sheep fence separated his land from Pa's, and a big black champion sheep named Bluetoe, leader of the flock, spent most of the day looking across the fence and watching Muley.

Muley had a habit of grazing near the fenceline where the grass was tall, and the big Bluetoe just dared her to come across the fence. There were times when old Muley stood with her head low and stared back at him with a promise that she one day would cross the fence and fight it out. I don't know who I feared the most, Tom Turner or Bluetoe. Old Bluetoe had always looked at me hoping that he would one day take out the seat of my britches.

Whenever I found fault with Pa's land, I closed my eyes and thought about his callused hands and wrinkled skin, and feeling low enough to crawl under a snake's belly, I asked forgiveness for my thoughts. Like Pa, I searched for the good streak in everything. Pa said it was there for any man who looked deep enough to find it. All in all, I figured it was a fair land for a boy to grow up on—especially with a good hound-dog in front of him. The rugged land offered cover for game. Most of the high points held fat coveys of quail that came up under my feet so quickly that they scared me. The small clear running branch that split the land in half added a softness to the red clay on either side. The soft earth close to the water sprouted tender shoots that the groundhogs loved to eat. The woods held squirrels, both red and gray, and once Pa had shot a white one and had taken it into town to show off. Foxes lived under the rock cliffs, some native to the land and others brought in by Tom Turner for his foxhounds to run. Bringing the foxes in was a bad thing. A few could be reckoned with since the silent hills had a way of keeping things on an even keel. But the little gray fox would run to his den after a short chase and the bigger reds would run all night. So Tom Turner heaped the hills with red foxes and they multiplied like berries on a wild berry bush. When the foxes weren't aggravating hounds, they searched the hills for young game and eggs to suck. Tom Turner's land offered little cover for them, so they crossed to Pa's land to live under the rock cliffs. They grew brazen enough to steal chickens hereabouts, and they had even snitched a few from Ma since there was no dog on the place to stop them. A true foxhunter didn't hunt to kill but only to hear his hounds on the trail, so the foxes had but one enemy, Hyford Ringtom.

Hyford Ringtom was the best friend I had, and he sure knew how to deal with a fox. He had lived in the hills until he was as old as the trees. He knew a lot about the law, too. He said that Pa had a right to do something about the foxes that Tom Turner had planted on his property. But Pa's land was free to all, people and varmints alike. So Hyford Ringtom wandered the hills alone, trying to rid the country of foxes.

I thought I would join him when I got my hound-dog. I was back thinking of the sort of dog I wanted and the sort of dog I ought to be mighty careful not to get. Mostly, there were two sorts that I did not want: Hyford Ringtom's little feist Rufus and Tom Turner's foxhounds. I had good reason. Just last year I was standing on the top of Crows Point with Hyford and Rufus on a squirrel hunt. It was hot; the woods were dry, and the walking was slow.

"If there be any squirrels about," Hyford says to me, "old Rufus will fetch'em out."

And that little dog, no bigger than a good-sized house cat, and gray like the hair of a possum with the tips of white on the ends, spent the better part of the morning tripping first me and then Hyford Ringtom. He was the most peculiar squirrel dog I ever saw. The only times he ranged ahead of us was when the path ahead of us was clear. If he came to a brier that had fallen across the path he just squatted there and waited for Hyford or me to bend down and hold it up for him to go under. He just seemed to expect it. And once the brier was high enough for him to get under he just went lickety-splitting through, paying no mind that he had knocked you off balance and caused the brier to swish you in the face keen enough to bring tears. While Hyford was picking the briers out of my face, he says to me: "Don't you ever get in the way of that Rufus dog. He will trample man or beast to get a squirrel." I watched the little dog range out to where another bush had fallen across the path. He kept his nose high in the air, high enough for a good rainstorm to drown him for sure.

"How does he ever trail game with his nose so high in the air?" I asked Hyford.

"Don't trail," Hyford said. "Just goes looking and winding. Got the eyes of a hawk and a nose like a divining rod. Look at him!" And the little feist went walking up the path lifting his paws high and setting them down as slow as a summer wind. I figured he was making sure he didn't pop them down on a rock or sawbrier. But Hyford grinned. "Sneaking up on 'em, he is. I've seen that Rufus sneak right up to the very tree, lock his legs around the trunk, shinny up and go right down the den hole after a squirrel."

Somehow that day the feist managed to get out of sight. I think he got lost and didn't have voice enough to let us know where he was. Well, I didn't have a chance to think about where he was for long. All of a sudden I looked up ahead and saw the biggest gray squirrel latched to a tree I had ever seen. I stopped and raised my rifle. The wind commenced blowing considerably, tangling spider webs over my eyes. Early in the morning, the woods are full of the night works of spiders and the wind blows the webs about and the early sun sparkles on them. When I raised the rifle a second time Hyford Ringtom was looking down the sights with me.

"Hold it!" he shouted, as nervous as the wind.

18

"Hold it! It's old Rufus!"

"But what's he doing fastened to the side of that tree?" I asked, not too sure that it was him but maybe a squirrel that Hyford was aiming to pop out ahead of me.

"He's going after a squirrel like I said he would," Hyford said.

"But don't he bark treed?" I asked, walking toward the tree with Hyford.

"Not on squirrels," Hyford said. "Don't want to give himself away by barking. Now, he opens some on foxes and the likes."

"But how do you know when he has treed a squirrel?" I asked.

"Just look till you find him clamped on the side of a tree," Hyford said. He shook his head. "Straddling them big trees has bowed the little feller's legs till he can hardly walk straight."

The gray squirrel was balled up near the top of that big black gum tree and the wind was swinging him back and forth.

"Shoot him out!" Hyford said. "Ain't no use in letting Rufus shinny all the way to the top."

But before I could pull the trigger on the rifle the little feist legs gave way and he slid down the tree to the ground. The squirrel heard the noise and dodged around a limb. I couldn't see him.

Well, we tried everything to make that squirrel move and give away his hiding place. Hyford marched around the tree making all sorts of weird noises hoping to make the squirrel move. Then, he stopped to whisper something in my ear. We would try to fool that squirrel into believing we had given up finding him. Hyford looked unconcerned and said to me: "Come on, Caleb, let's go. That squirrel has done left the tree."

We walked off a few steps and I turned quick to shoot. The squirrel went lickety-splitting out of the top of the black gum. He crossed to a hickory sapling was preparing to spring into a den oak, when I tumbled him out. I started after him knowing full well that he could get tangled up among the leaves on the ground and I'd never be able to find him. Hyford grabbed me by the arm.

"Hold it," he said, pushing out his chest and drawing his lips like you do when you intend to do a smart of bragging. "I see you ain't used to hunting with a good squirrel dog, son. Let Rufus fetch that squirrel for you. That dog plumb takes the work out of hunting. Best retriever in the Big Sandy Valley."

The little feist trailed off to where the squirrel fell.

"Hear there! Hi there! Who-o-o-o-o!" I screamed after him.

But before I could reach that Rufus dog he had jerked the hide from the squirrel and gulped half of him down.

"'Pon my word!" Hyford said. "Never knowed that Rufus dog to do a thing like that. Reckon I'll have to talk to him about it."

Later Hyford tried hard to make amends for what Rufus had done. He claimed that the squirrel had been eating pine cones and had the strength of pine in his meat which would make him too strong to eat. There was truth in this. A squirrel was no good to eat when it ate pine cones. The pine sure enough would scent its meat, making it no good. Hyford said that Rufus did not believe in letting game go to waste. But I kept my thinking to myself. That Rufus was high on my list of don't-want-dogs. He was a little feist dog with his legs bowed so bad from straddling trees you could have rolled a hoop between them, and a he was a squirrel eater, too!

I couldn't say much for a foxhound, either. A hound-dog, to my way of figuring, was put here to take game, not just for running the very tail off a fox with no intentions of catching him.

But in my room at night, far off I could hear Tom Turner's foxhound bawl fox. All of a sudden, the pack went up and down the sides of the mountains, and the chase was on. Their voices bounced from the sides of the mountains and trailed to my room like it had been mellowed by a long trip through a hollow log, soft and pretty. Closer . . . closer . . . closer, bursting right down the slopes behind the house until the deep bawls just seemed to shake the very rafters of my room. The moon would be full and hanging over the earth like the globe of a lantern. Often I watched the pack turn the fox down the mountain and then back up the other side, and under the softness of the moon the hounds seemed to be moving in slow motion. Always a little speckled gyp was leading the pack of hounds.

Long, lean and shallow-chested, the foxhound was made for running. Hyford Ringtom once said that an old foxhound too slow to run with a pack made about the best tree dog. But, all in all, the foxhound belonged to a trifling man . . . one that wanted to build a fire along a mountain top and argue that it was his dog leading the chase. No sir, a foxhound just wouldn't do for me. They had the looks. I won't deny that. But they only ran at night and then laid around during the day. I wanted a day dog as well as a night dog . . . one to get real close to . . . to confide in and whisper secrets in his ear, secrets that I wouldn't even tell Hyford Ringtom, as close as we were.

And yet, I just can't talk bad about foxhounds without feeling a little guilty. For there were times when I favored owning the little speckled gyp, Nellie Bell, that led the pack of hounds. Hyford Ringtom spoke of her as being the best foxhound in Kentucky. She owned about as many ribbons for hunting as old Bluetoe had won as a champion ram. Once she won a big fox chase down in Tennessee.

I thought, at the time, if she were mine she would not run foxes. I'd set right out to break her. I thought I'd just start right off by saying to her: "I won't cater to your running a trifling fox, Nellie Bell." I'd fill her bed with more fox scent than she could sniff up on a thousand and one chases. I'd make her sick of smelling fox scent.

I'd only been real close to Nellie Bell once. I was on top of a point after a mess of squirrel when she came lickety-splitting across a bed of dry leaves. She saw me and stopped, stood there tired and sore from running fox all night. Dawn had just popped out of the sky and was still shaking some night from it. The little gyp wagged her tail, which made me feel right proud for some reason. I clicked my lips and coaxed her toward me.

"Don't you know not to coax another man's hound!" a deep voice yelled and I began to shake worse than an autumn leaf in a high wind.

Tom Turner stood near his sheep fence with a snap chain in one hand. The small gyp heard his voice and dropped to her belly and crawled off toward him like she had done something wrong. He snapped the chain to her collar and jerked her to her feet. "Won't you ever learn to quit with the rest of the pack!" he scolded.

The small gyp whimpered and I was afraid to say anything. Finally I took a deep breath and said:

"She sure is a right pretty sight."

"Best foxhound in these hills," he said, more to the hound than to me. He set his eyes on the rifle over the crook of my arm. "Your Pa turn you loose with that rifle, no bigger than you are? Well, just make sure you don't fire that gun across my fenceline. I got sheep over here!"

Tom Turner shamed me by saying that. I figured to be about as good as Pa with a rifle. If Tom Turner would have looked at the two big gray squirrels hanging from my belt he would have known that. And as for firing a bullet across his fenceline . . . what about Nellie Bell coming across Pa's land lickety-splitting, scaring the squirrels. Pa's land was free and I didn't hold it against the little gyp for crossing the land, scaring the squirrels. Two squirrels were enough for a meal anyway. Ma would call me wasteful if I killed more than two.

There was a good streak in every man, Pa said. But on my way back down the mountain I wondered how he could ever find one in Tom Turner.

Chapter Three

Closer to the end of the month the days became almost unbearable. It was three days before the stock sales began when I finally decided on the sort of dog I wanted. It happened this way: Thinking that I would get a hound-dog, I got to bragging. One evening I stuck my thumbs in the front of my britches and set off toward Hyford Ringtom's as happy as if I had the whole world shriveled up no bigger than a sycamore ball and tucked in my back pocket.

This time of the evening, I knew I would find Hyford sitting on the front porch of his one-room cabin twirling his crooked finger in the air like he was trying to pull down the last warm touch of spring sun. Actually he would be talking to Rufus, who would be stretched out beside him scratching fleas. Ma said that Rufus did not have enough getup about him to scratch his own fleas. She reckoned, and had even said so, that if Hyford ever caught a crop of fleas he would have been too shiftless to scratch them—probably would have talked someone else into scratching them for him. For Ma, Hyford was about as lowdown as they came. He had managed to live for the better part of seventy years in a one-room cabin without having to cook a meal. She said old women marched their daughters past his cabin pointing crooked fingers and warning their daughters that this was the kind of man they might end up marrying if they didn't mind their elders. Some brought boys too, telling them that they just might grow up to be like Hyford. Ma never marched me past his cabin. I think that she knew all along that I wanted, more than anything, to be just like Hyford Ringtom.

Pa just laughed at Hyford's ways, especially the way he managed to get free meals. Hyford visited most places just often enough to get a free meal and not too much to aggravate the womenfolks. He came to our house about twice a week, which was more often than any other place, and he fooled Ma every time. Of course, Hyford and Pa had been friends for a long time. He would wipe the sweat from his face when he walked into the yard. "Well, Mrs. Tate," he would say, "just can't stay as long as I'd like this trip. Me and this Rufus dog have been hunting foxes in the hills all day. Now . . . there ain't rightly any reason why I should be out hunting foxes. Hide ain't worth anything and there is no bounty on 'em either." Then he would lean close and squeeze out a tear, something he could do every time. "But I just can't stand by idle and know them foxes are a-stealing my neighbors' chickens. I dearly love my friends. And just as long as me and old Rufus can totter through these hills, I aim to take a toll of 'em." Rufus would traipse on off toward the henhouse, looking for a meal which would most likely be an egg to suck from Ma's henhouse, Hyford explaining later that the small hole in the wire was made during the night by a fox, and Ma would swear that she hadn't noticed the hole earlier in the day. "The trail of that particular fox is mighty cold by now, but old Rufus might be able to pick it up." The scent of the evening meal would drift out of the kitchen. "Now don't you let me and this Rufus dog keep you from your vittles, Mrs. Tate," he would say. He would look out as the evening sun topped the corn patch and shake his head in disbelief. "My, is it that late? Reckon I ought to be getting on home. No, thank you, I won't stay for supper this trip. Didn't aim to stop at mealtime. Just thought I'd ask, being over this way, to see if the foxes had been pestering you . . . no dog on the place and such. I'll scratch me out a few berries and roots on the way back over the mountain. It don't take much to feed an old shriveled-up man like me." He would twirl his nose and sniff like a hound-dog. "You know, Mrs. Tate, there ain't a woman in these hills that can set a table like you. You just put 'em to shame with your cooking." A little brag-ging on Ma and she softened like the summer shell of a crawdad. "Now, Mrs. Tate, I just weren't aiming to stop to eat, but I ain't going to turn down your invite and hurt your feelings. I hope you ain't gone to no special trouble for old Hyford. I ain't really hungry at all, but I will be obliged to take something to drink, and a bone for old Rufus if there is meat on the table."

Hyford Ringtom could eat more than the three of us, and he usually did. When he had finished, he for-got all about hunting fox. He sprawled out on the floor in the living room and spit amber toward the grate, mostly missing. Ma always fussed; that is, until he turned to brag on her dress or something she was wear-ing. I always sprawled out beside him and took in his talk of the hills like parched clay could gulp down a spring rain.

I sat on the porch that evening and talked to Hyford until the shadows crossed the peaks of the mountains like black furrows of earth.

"Yep," Hyford says to me, "you just make sure you take that saddleback runt and trade for a little teeny dog. A teeny dog has a way of sneaking inside a feller's chest and making the old ticker speed up."

"I ain't rightly made up my mind yet," I told Hyford. And to be honest, I was thinking that I was just not too well pleased with that Rufus dog. I just didn't know whether or not so much hound could be crammed into such a tiny wad without it being a mite unbalanced. His voice was no louder than the yip of a gray fox.

"Man tones his ear to the bark of his dog," Hyford said. "Size ain't got nothing to do with a bark anyways. If you think it has then just how do you account for the croak of a bullfrog? He bellers like a bull and ain't no bigger than a fist. And who would ever guess that a little old acorn held an oak tree inside it? Here's the straight of it: There's two common sorts of dogs. Little dogs, and big dogs. And then there's old Rufus."

"But ain't Rufus a little dog?" I asked.

"Not rightly," Hyford said. "He is a once-in-a-life-time-dog . . . a cross between a ferret and a feist. Runs game in the hole and goes in after it. Burrows through them dark tunnels like a snake. I wouldn't be degrading Rufus by classing him with any of the two common types of dogs."

Hyford Ringtom's words weren't to be tossed aside like shucks from an ear of corn. There wasn't another man with his knowledge of the hill country. Pa was closest. When it came to dogs, they agreed that looks didn't count much. Each knew that a lot could be crammed inside a small heart.

But I think what really made me decide I would bargain for a small dog was the "sneaking ways" Hyford claimed a little dog was bound to have. I could just see a teeny dog sneaking on past Ma and crawling into bed with me at night. He would just plain fool her into believing he was under the floor, where Big Joe once slept.

Chapter Four

The morning of the stock sales, I was overjoyed. I was so excited, I jumped off the ground and kicked my heels together. I felt so good that I believed I could out-bargain old Billy Flint.

Billy Flint was as much a part of the stock sales as the brutes that were sold there. He came to bargain and that was all. He just purely loved skinning a man. And he was ready to swap anything from a talking crow to a groundhog. He was willing to spend fifty dollars to build a set of teeth for an old mule just to trade it and make someone believe it was a two-year-old. Hyford Ringtom had once watched Billy Flint trade a city fellow a mule, and the city fellow was living in an apartment house, with no more need of a mule than a pocketful of rattlesnakes. Billy Flint had talked as smooth as a summer wind. Not only had he got the swap across, but he had also managed to take the city fellow's little house dog and twenty dollars to boot. Suddenly it dawned on the city fellow that he had no place or use for a mule, and he was bound to have a hard time explaining to his wife what had happened to her little dog. So he tried to sell Billy Flint the mule back. Then he offered to trade back even for the dog. "Trade you a champion squirrel dog for that old mule!" Billy Flint said, insulted.

"Squirrel dog!" the city fellow said. "Why, that little dog has never been farther than the end of his lead chain. Never been in the hills in his life."

Well, before it all ended, Billy Flint had his mule back, and had sold the dog back to the city fellow, making him believe that he had got himself the best squirrel dog in the country. And he got twenty dollars to boot!

The stock sales were the market place for almost everything. You could be sure that there would be hound-dogs for sale. A good hound-dog was as precious as a wife, as far as I was concerned. I didn't care much for women.

Pa always found a ready market for his hogs. Hogs prospered on Pa's rugged land, and spring was the best time to sell them. They could then be fattened over the summer, so they would be ready for slaughter when the weather was cold enough to preserve meat.

I had been up for hours, and daylight still hid among the hills. While I harnessed old Bossin, Pa ran his shoats up into the wagon and Pa said: "We'll put this runt saddleback in a sack. Just let its head stick out for air. You'll be able to carry it at the sales to wherever they are bargaining off dogs." He looked at me for the first time with concern on his face. "And Caleb, being as how we are going to have a dog on the place, try to pick a pretty one. It will please your ma . . ."

"I'll get the prettiest one at the sales," I said.

Ma and Pa did little talking as we neared town. I figured him to be busy setting the price that he would ask for his shoats, and I was thinking just how I would strike my bargain for a hound-dog:

Well now, gentlemen, I would say, this here little saddleback is the prize of Pa's shoats. I don't need to waste time telling you what sort of hogs Pa raises. Best in the hill country. Yes, this one is a mite small. But it is as solid as a rock. And any good hog man knows a runt has sweeter meat. Why, once they take a mind to grow they are apt to bust their hides with bigness. Now, you don't expect me to trade a shoat like this for a mangy pup! Let's see the best you got. (Then I'd drop down on my knees and look at the pretty pups.)

I'd look for broadness between the ears. I'd expect a deep chest, long ears and solid teeth, although I knew that a pup's teeth didn't count much since he'd get better ones with age. But it seemed to me that to do so would prove that I was an expert on hound-dogs. Color didn't count much with me, but since Pa had said looks were important to Ma, I figured to pick a good-colored one.

It was easy thinking of all these things until we came into sight of the stockyards. Then I couldn't think of anything, because I had a bad case of the jitters. I was almost as confused as that saddleback runt in the sack.

Closer to the yards, we pulled in behind a long line of wagons and edged inch by inch toward the stockyards. The wagons were filled with every kind of brute and fowl native to the hill country: cows, hogs, sheep, chickens, turkeys, ducks, geese, and guineas. Here and there a horse or mule, hitched to the end of a wagon had been brought in to sell.

The wagons all moved toward a board ramp where they could be unloaded, and the cargoes were put in stalls to be bargained. It was the noisiest place I'd ever been. Men walked out to meet the wagons, carrying long prodding sticks to turn the animals so they could see both sides. Some bargains were struck right then and there, and these wagons were pulled out of the line and never reached the stockyards. We pulled up to the unloading ramp. Pa looked at me and grinned.

"Feel like bargaining, son?" he said.

"Just like I could beat old Billy Flint," I said.

Pa grinned wider. "Just make sure you don't bargain with Billy Flint. That's the first thing a good bargainer learns." He helped me get the runt into my arms.

"You're on your own now. I'll meet you and that pretty hound pup back at the wagon."

I started up through the winding paths that wound between stall pens on either side, the saddleback runt squealing like I was sticking it with a thorn.

"That shoat cold or something?" asked an old man, gathered in a group of others who pointed a crooked finger at me. My face smarted.

"Naw," another said, "he's just put clothes on 'im, seems to me."

I got to thinking about my face smarting. I knew for sure that I couldn't expect to hide as big a thing as a runt shoat in a sack. And I couldn't be acting like a greenhorn by letting my face smart. Once a greenhorn was spotted at the sales, old men followed them around knowing they might well skin them alive in a trade.

I just couldn't find where the hound-dogs were being bargained. I was afraid to ask. To have to ask might show that I was somewhat new to the sales. And so I just blundered on, lost and looking.

But after a long while, I decided I must ask or take the chance of carrying the shoat back to the wagon without a trade. I picked out an old man near the corner of the yards. His skin was wrinkled like a summer potato and his beard was long and white like a billy goat's. I figured he wouldn't have much use for a saddleback runt. I walked right up to him:

"Where are the hound-dogs today?" I asked. "They just keep moving them around from place to place until a fellow don't know from one sale to the other where to look."

"You're right," he said. "Stock just keeps moving the smaller animals back. Dogs are at the far end of the yard today, near that open field there. Billy Flint's up there with a big pack. Fine-looking hounds . . . leastways on the outside."

"Well," I says, "I don't aim to bargain with Billy Flint. Where else might they be bargaining hound-dogs?"

"Ain't bargaining hound-dogs no other place," he says. "Heard Billy Flint bought them today before they reached the auction block. You'll trade with him or go home empty handed."

I honestly intended, right then and there, to head back to the wagon. But the deep bawl of a hound stopped me. It drowned out all the other noises of the yards and hung in my ears for time on end. And as I moved toward the open field, I intended to just look around. That was all. First thing I knew I was standing right there in a circle of men, facing Billy Flint.

From the innocent look in Billy Flint's eyes, a man would never have guessed him to be a trader. His voice was as fast and smooth as the wild turkey caller Hyford Ringtom had made last year. He reached down and jerked a big black-and-tan hound upon the block beside him. He pointed at a man close to the block.

"What do you see here beside me, brother?" he asked.

"Hound-dog," the man said, spitting amber into the grass. "Didn't that hound belong to Diddle Tuffs? Runs a fox now and then, hear tell."

"Talk lower!" Billy Flint said in a whisper that took a close ear to catch it. "Do you want to hurt the feeling of a great hound-dog? This, my friends, just happened to be the second cousin to the old champ himself, Beating Drum. And any man that says he ain't familiar with the old champ Beating Drum don't know a straw about hound-dogs. Now, what about that!" He pointed to the same man again.

The man squinted and looked guilty. "I got the wrong dog for sure," he said. "That sure ain't the one that belonged to Diddle Tuffs. And that Beating Drum was a great one, for sure."

And that's about what I would have said, had he asked me. Hyford Ringtom had known all the great dogs hereabouts and I had never heard him say anything about a dog named Beating Drum. But dadgum if I'da said I didn't know him here in this crowd and shown that I didn't know a straw about hound-dogs, especially a champion.

Billy Flint talked faster, stopping only long enough

to allow his praise to drift through the crowd and take hold. But he had already said enough for me!

"One saddleback shoat!" I tried to holler above the other bids. I was so fired up I had to say something.

"Step back, son," Billy Flint said. "Don't crowd these men that are about to skin old Billy Flint on this hound. People always told me I was too big-hearted to be in this business. But I don't mind losing. I like to make people happy."

The big hound sold before I could strike my bid again. And a big bluetick went next. A fine-looking hound that could do everything but stretch game out on a board, and he was willing to try that, according to Billy Flint, but by gum I believed him. How much for this one? he said.

"One saddleback shoat!" I shouted.

"Stand back now, son!" Billy Flint said, jerking another hound upon the block. And I wished a thousand and one times I had taken one of the bigger shoats. The runt just kept squealing above everything, making me ashamed to no end. Finally Billy Flint leaned over toward me and said:

"Great day in the morning, son, can't you keep that sick pig quiet? He's got these hounds so nervous they will hardly stand on the block. They're quivering like they got distemper or something of the like!"

The more I tried to comfort that pig the more it

squealed.

"Great day!" Billy Flint said again. "I never heard a pig with a squealer like that. Is it sick or something?"

"No sir, " I said, "this here saddleback is the prize of Pa's . . ." Billy Flint turned around and was halfway through auctioning off another hound, paying no attention to me whatsoever. I bid on that hound, too. Fact is, I just kept bidding on and on. And the faster the hounds went off the block the lower my heart sank. The crowd began to scatter, thinking that Billy Flint had just sold the last of the lot. I felt downcast, almost ashamed to go back to the wagon. I mingled off with the crowd, still trying to quiet that infernal pig.

"Wait!"

Billy Flint's voice stopped me in my tracks. I turned with the crowd to look.

"Hold everything!" Billy Flint shouted. "It has long been my custom at the end of a bargaining day to make someone a real prize . . . sorta stretch my big heart for all it's worth. I'm stretching it today, gentlemen, clear out of shape."

And the next thing I knew I was staring into the eyes of a big rusty dog. It looked to be a cur. The coat on the big rangy dog favored that of an airedale, with years of traipsing the sawbrier country marking it well. In places the hair had been pulled off short and did not sprout back, exposing his old rusty hide. There was little or no hair left on his muzzle as far as his floppy ears. I should say ear, since one of them appeared to be half chewed off. His coat was all brown, except for a touch of misty gray near his eyes. I thought at the time that the touch of misty gray might have told his years of living here in the hill country, but I could not be sure since I did not know if the hair of a dog grayed with age, like the hair on the head and face of an old man, like Hyford Ringtom. He was sure an odd-looking brute. The crowd around laughed and I joined them.

"This is worth waiting to see," a man next to me said. "I've watched old Billy Flint make many a bargain. I've seen him sell a hound, buy it back, and sell it among the same crowd for double his money. But I'd like to see what he can do with that sack of skin and bones there on the block beside him. Fact is, I'd like to see him give it away. I do believe old Billy Flint has gone too far this time."

I sorta threw my shoulders back and said right big: "I'd like to see him rid himself of that one myself."

"Gentlemen," Billy Flint said, in a voice sad enough to bring rain, "I'm going to be honest with you. Here, on this block beside me, stands the greatest varmint catcher of them all . . . small varmints now, since he has aged a little." He jerked his head and looked solemn like he would be apt to shoot the next man that showed his teeth. "Don't laugh!" The big dog flopped down on his haunches. Billy Flint jerked him hard to his feet and the old dog whimpered. "Git up!" he scolded. He jerked the old dog so hard with the rope around his neck that he cut off his wind and the old fellow gulped for breath. He lowered his ugly head and squinted with pain like when you strike your finger with a hammer. The men about laughed louder and waited to see if Billy Flint was going to be able to keep the old dog standing. I forced a laugh, too. But it was sure enough forced. I tell you right now that the whimper of that old dog had a way of sneaking under a fellow's skin. I wouldn't want you to think that I was going soft at the time, though. "Please hold your laughs out of respect." Billy Flint was talking again. "Truth be what it is, you have a champion before you. Got a little age now, and brings to this block a few faults. He was just too much hound to ever run with a pack. Just seemed to be searching all these years for a master that he could hunt his heart out for. And as far as I know he is still searching today. Just look at him stand!"

The big dog had squatted to his rear again. And this time Billy Flint hit him hard with a prodding stick. The big dog yelped and stuck his long tail between his legs. His big watery eyes crossed mine and hung there for a moment. He was a sorry-looking sight, but he didn't need to be looking to me for any sympathy.

"Crippled in the hindquarters, ain't he?" a man

43

asked.

"Don't interrupt me while I am trying to explain that," Billy Flint said. "I wouldn't want anyone here thinking that old Billy Flint was trying to put a crippled dog off on anyone. Yes, sir, that's right. He's crippled a mite in one hind leg." He pointed to the crippled leg with the tip of the prodding stick. "You can see this leg has a slight bow in it. But allow me to tell you how it got that bow. Chased a mountain lion right off a cliff not too far from here. Yes sir, that's just what he did. A real honest-to-goodness mountain lion. The only mountain lion I reckon to ever be here in these hills. Got loose from a circus some years ago. Wasn't a hound-dog in this country that would trail it. The big lion just went around killing cattle by the herds. What do you think of that! Just might be killing today if it weren't for this old dog. Chased it all alone, he did, through the day and the dark. Rode its back right over a high cliff and had it killed before they reached the ground. Landed on a rock, he did, and busted this leg." Billy Flint's voice took a quiver to it. "Saved all the cattle and the little calves, bless their hearts. Now laugh, gentlemen." Billy Flint pulled his handkerchief from his pocket. The crowd grew solemn.

"Billy Flint ought to have been a preacher," a man said next to me.

"Couldn't keep from lying," a man answered him.

"That sack of old bones would be apt to run from a field mouse and he knows it."

"Notice the hair," Billy Flint said. "See the airedale here! Let me remind you, gentlemen, that this is the breed of dog they use to hunt mountain lions with out in the West. What am I bid? One a time, please!"

The old dog squatted again and this time Billy Flint hit him good and hard. The old dog trembled with the blow. And for some reason, he just hunkered like an old man whipped with age and too helpless to fight back. Tears came from his sad eyes. I never before knew that tears could come from the eyes of an old dog. He just set his big, ugly eyes on mine and I thought I saw his tail wagging. Well, I had to do something. I pinched the saddleback runt and he squealed to high heavens.

"What am I bid?" Billy Flint asked again.

Now just what would Pa be apt to think, I thought, if I was to come dragging a dog like that back to the wagon? I flinched as Billy Flint struck him again.

"Well," Billy Flint said, in a more pleading voice, "maybe he ain't much to look at. I ain't offering him as a pretty picture. But, given the right master, he's apt to be the greatest varmint catcher in this country. A prize to keep the smaller varmints away from the house while the younger dogs are out in the hills hunting."

The big dog just stood there trembling, with nobody wanting him. The crowd laughed loud enough to almost drown the squeal of my pig. They mocked him and teased him, making a fool of him and Billy Flint as well. There just wasn't any cause I could see for treating the old dog like that. Then I got to thinking of the things Pa had told me about dogs at the stock sales. About some being sold and some not. The ones that did not sell were not considered worth taking home by their owners. They could not be brought back and sold another time, generally. Most times they were left to wander around the stockyards, into the streets and into the paths of automobiles. Sometimes they wandered about with nothing to eat until they starved to death. Sometimes they became so thick around town that they gathered in half-wild packs and had to be shot down. It was bad enough to die, I reckoned, worse to die without even being wanted.

And yet he was the ugliest and saddest-looking brute I had ever set my eyes on. Just stood there a laughing-stock, trembling and dodging the prodding stick, so confused he didn't know what to do. And Billy Flint was mad now. He hit the old dog hard enough to cause him to loose footing.

"Stand!" he shouted. "Don't squat there and make a fool of me!"

"Don't!" I shouted. "Don't hit him again. Please!"

Billy Flint cocked his ear and looked down at me. He let his eyes wander to the saddleback shoat. The rest of the crowd stared at me now as if to say everything was between me and Billy Flint. I began to feel uneasy, like I was now the difference between Billy Flint being the laughingstock of the sales . . . or me.

"Did I hear you bid, son?" he asked.

Suddenly I couldn't hear a sound coming from the whole stockyard. I knew that the brutes must still be there carrying on just as much as before. But I just couldn't seem to hear them. I couldn't even hear the squeal of the shoat, and I knew for sure that it still squealed because a man next to me held his ears.

"No . . . nope!" I answered.

"Then don't be telling me what I can or cannot do with this dog!" he said. "Stand up there, you old tramp!"

The big dog dropped with the blow and scooted across the block on his belly, looking up at me with his sad eyes, whimpering and finally pushing his nose into the palm of my hand. And to save me I just don't know how my hand got over on the block to meet him. And what made my hand move over his old ugly coat, causing men around me to laugh, and a smile to come on the face of Billy Flint? I felt the big welt that the prodding stick had made, and I heard the thumping of the big dog's tail. He wasn't much to look at.

Billy Flint raised the prodding stick again. I looked up and saw it swimming around through the tears in my eyes. I felt the ugly dog tremble and tighten to take the blow that he knew was coming for what he had done. I looked up at Billy Flint.

"One saddleback shoat!" I said.

"Sold for a pig in a poke," Billy Flint laughed.

I guess I was dazed. Here I stood, alone now, the big, ugly dog by my side. I could still hear Billy Flint as he bargained off my runt shoat: "What am I bid, gentlemen? This saddleback is the prize of the litter. Apt to grow out of its hide once it takes a notion . . ."

Well, here I was. I didn't have me a dog and the shoat was gone. There wasn't anything to be happy about. I didn't know how I would explain it to Pa: How I had gone soft on a big, ugly brute that I was ashamed to bring back to the wagon and had bought his freedom with the saddleback runt. I would turn the big dog loose. Maybe he would get killed by an automobile, starve to death, or have to be shot. But at least he stood a chance this way. He wouldn't go down under blows from Billy Flint, or have to squat there in front of a bunch of men, to be whipped and laughed at.

I turned toward the wagon. And don't you know that that big ugly brute was right there beside me, hugging as close to my britches as bark to a tree! Didn't he know that things were bad enough as it was? I had bargained with Billy Flint and got skinned alive! Just what I told Pa I would be sure not to do. Now, just where did the big dog think he was going? Not close enough for Pa to see him, that was for sure. Big paws almost as large as Rufus's head; an old ugly dog with the better part of his life gone. I bet he even had fleas.

I was so shamed that I thought once of just not going back to the wagon at all. I would just wander off like an unwanted dog. But there was nowhere to go.

I tried hard to get rid of that ugly dog, but he followed me around the stockyards like I had raised him from a pup. I sat down and tried to think. The big dog limped over and lay his ugly head across my lap. He looked up at me with his sad eyes as if to say that from here on in he didn't have a worry in this world. I just sorta let my hand wander over his coat again. The welts were still there. I stood up and pointed my finger:

"You got your freedom, big dog! Now, git!"

The big dog lowered his head and walked off a ways. And then he turned and looked back as if he thought I didn't mean what I had said.

"Go on!" I said.

He turned and limped a piece farther. He turned and looked back again.

Now just where does he think he is going? I said to myself. Ain't he got sense enough to know that the way he is heading leads nowhere? Don't he know that there ain't ever going to be a place for him to go? That nobody wants a big, ugly dog like him? Ma wouldn't allow him on the place. Pa wouldn't allow him to ride the wagon. Hyford Ringtom wouldn't want him close to Rufus. "You just limp off, old ugly dog, and I'll try to make my peace with Pa for losing the shoat!"

And still he stood there, staring as if he was waiting for me to make up my mind. All of a sudden, I was thinking about the many talks me and Pa had had. He wouldn't try to tell me how to bargain, he said. And I thought of the words of Billy Flint, how the dog was apt to be the greatest varmint dog in the country. . . one to keep hill varmints away from the house. Wasn't this the reason Ma had consented to having a dog on the place? And I thought of the day old Rufus had stolen that squirrel from me. I didn't have to take Billy Flint's word that an airedale was used in the West to hunt mountain lions. I had heard Hyford Ringtom say that.

I was measuring the streaks in the old dog now. Truth was I had made my bargain. And for better or worse, I ought to be man enough to stick with it. He did have airedale in him. And they did hunt mountain lions with his sort out West. Well, to be right truthful about it, I just didn't think I would want a little dog that could be whipped by a groundhog, maybe. I took a real good look at that old dog. He wagged his tail as keen as a branch in a windstorm.

"Come on, big dog," I said, "let's go home."

He came padding along beside me toward the wagon.

Chapter Five

Pa was not yet back at the wagon when we got there. I went to the rear of it and lowered the tailgate and reached down to help the big dog up. He just looked at me with his sorry eyes and walked off like he was just plain disgusted with me. And the next thing I knew he went sailing through the air like a bird. He lit in the bed of the wagon and went tumbling over himself until he hit the front seat. He pulled himself up and looked at me.

Old Bossin felt the jolt of the wagon and looked around to see what had made it. He looked the big dog square in the eyes and heehawed as loud as he could. The big dog curled his upper lip and a low growl came from deep in his throat. Old Bossin turned around to mind his own business then.

"Thataboy, big dog," I said. "You and old Bossin are apt to get along now. You just showed him you were to be reckoned with. That's the only way to treat a mule;

show him who's the boss right off. But . . . just don't you go letting Pa see you acting so brazen, leastways until after he has got to know you better. He is apt to think you are just plumb impudent." And the big dog thumped his tail on the floor boards of the wagon.

I just didn't know how Pa was apt to take to the big dog. He just might start stripping merits from him left and right. And it would be my place to add them back just as fast. A lot depended on how badly I wanted the ugly dog. I reckon he had little else in his favor. But there was a chance that Pa might just look right on through the hide of the old dog and see all the goodness inside. A real hound-dog man could do that. Pa would not be apt to make fun. For once, I was glad that Pa was a man to find a good streak in anything. If he found one in Tom Turner he ought to find one in the big dog as broad as a mountain, goodness just busting from his rusty hide. Well, I wouldn't have long to wait. Pa was walking toward the wagon.

I guess it was only natural for him to stop and stare at the ugly dog as he pulled himself up into the wagon seat. I just set my teeth solid and stared right back at him. Pa stared another moment and then clicked his mouth to let old Bossin know we were ready to go home. He had never said a word, for good or bad, and I just looked around like it were a common thing for the big, ugly dog to be there in the wagon. Fact is, we were more than halfway home before Pa said to me:

"I guess you know what you got?"

"Reckon I do," I answered.

"Even swap?" he asked.

"Maybe to one man's way of thinking," I answered.

He stopped the wagon and looked back toward the stock sales. A cold chill swept over me. I knew there was still time to go back there.

"Trade with old Billy Flint?" Pa asked, starting the wagon.

"Beat him bad, Pa," I said. "Beat him good and proper in front of a big crowd of men."

Pa commenced a-laughing. He reached back then and patted the old dog on top of the head. The big dog took right up with him.

"Maybe you did at that," he said. "You feeling that way could make it so. Got airedale in him, ain't he? That's the kind they hunt mountain lions with out West, you know." Then Pa rubbed his hand over the crook in the big dog's hind leg.

"Nothing but a little bow there," I said right fast. "Don't bother him none at all. You ought to have seen that big dog jump into the wagon bed. Just like a bird!"

Pa studied the happiness in my face. I reckon it had been a spell since he had seen so much of it there. His eyes softened on the old dog.

"You don't have to add merits to the old dog for

54

my satisfaction," he said. "Your choice is good enough for me. But . . . we might as well be honest with one another. It ain't me you will have to please and you know it. It's your Ma. And you know that there are times that she can be stubborn as old Bossin. You won't have it easy pacifying her with that dog. And she ain't apt to judge him like a hound-dog man. She is apt to see no farther than his shaggy coat. And we might as well admit that he ain't got much there to show."

"I reckon he ain't at that, Pa," I answered. "Reckon I ain't got much in favor when it comes to influencing women either, Pa. I guess I was sorta leaning heavy on you when it came to Ma."

Pa stared at me with a stern face. And then he broke into a chuckle. "Something, I suppose, like I handled that old muley cow?"

"'Bout like that," I answered.

"Well," Pa said, "I'd be apt to start her off with this." He handed me a wrapped package. I peeked inside to see the new cloth that she had been wanting to make a dress.

"I guess from there on you are apt to be on your own," he said.

"But, Pa," I said. "You know Ma better than me."

"That I do," he answered. "That's why I'm leaving it up to you. She just might figure I'm old enough to know better."

I studied Pa's face for a moment.

"You wouldn't be trying to take merits from this big dog, would you, Pa?" I asked.

"Like I said," Pa answered, "them's the kind they use to hunt mountain lions with out West. Now there's a big streak of good in that old brute. And I'd say you better find it in front of Ma. Maybe you can make her believe there are mountain lions in the country about." Pa broke off into a laugh.

By the time we reached home a drizzle of rain fell. It seemed as if the very weather itself was against me. The rain fell on the big dog parting his hair right down his backbone, making it lay over like Hyford Ringtom's hair after he had plastered it down with groundhog grease and gone to fiddle at a square dancing. And Ma never cared much for the likes of that.

While Pa unharnessed and took old Bossin to the barn, I made my way across the yard with the big, ugly dog limping along beside me. I got to figuring it best to leave him outside until I checked to see the sort of humor Ma was in, and sorta bring her around with the bundle of new cloth.

"You stay," I said, being right pleased when the big dog squatted there in the rain like I had told him to do. I cracked the door then and stepped in out of the rain. Ma was there to meet me. But of a sudden she wasn't looking at me or the bundle under my arm at all; she

was staring toward the door that was still cracked open. I heard the squeak of the hinges and the patter of feet too quick and light to be Pa's. Ma placed her hands on her hips like she always did whenever she was looking at something with displeasure. She shook her head.

I looked slowly behind me. There he stood, the big dog in the doorway, water dripping from his ugly coat, lessening his chances of staying with every drop, being as how they fell on Ma's new braided rug—the one she had worked on all winter. I squinted my eyes. Big dog, I thought, if you have ever looked sadder in your whole life it had better be now if you are planning to stay with me. Maybe your humble looks will win Ma's heart. But he just thumped his long tail, offering no help at all. Just stood there looking up at her like he was as pretty as a picture.

"He's . . . he's . . . the sort of dog they hunt mountain lions with out in the West, Ma," I said, convincing as I could.

"Where on this earth did you find that thing!" she asked. Then she caught her breath. "You did find him, didn't you, Caleb? He did just follow you home."

"No ma'am," I said.

"You didn't . . . you couldn't have . . . not the saddleback shoat?" she asked.

"Yes ma'am," I said.

"Well," she said, "you could have sifted the mountains with a hayfork and never turned up a more sorry-looking sight than this."

"But he is the greatest varmint catcher of them all, Ma," I said.

Ma just frowned and shook her head as if to say she favored the hill varmints over the old dog. "There is nothing wrong in your wanting a dog, Caleb," she said. "Such is the way of all menfolk. But why this one? A discarded dog this old is bound to have many faults. You don't need an old dog. You need a young one. This dog is as old as you or older. And besides . . . he's a cripple. I do not hold fault against afflictions, but the crippled leg will hinder him. You know that. I thought you wanted a hunting dog?"

"He is a hunting dog, Ma," I said.

"He is a total outcast!" she said. "A mismatch! The big dog stays until the rains stop, and then you and your Pa can just traipse him right back to the stockyards. If possible you just bargain for a younger dog; a much prettier one." She shook her head. "This dog is just an old outcast!"

Chapter Six

The night was miserable. It rained slowly. Its soft patter on the roof was a sign that it would be lucky to last until morning. Back to the stock sales when the rain stops," Ma had said. Her words kept tumbling through my mind.

The big dog had slipped inside the small hole on the side of the house and followed the tunnel to the bed Big Joe had made under my room. Pa had grinned when the big dog had crawled into the hole. "Makes himself as welcomed around here as Hyford Ringtom," he said. "Well, he's bit off quite a chaw, thinking he is doing enough to claim old Joe's bed."

I was proud that Pa had compared the old dog to Hyford Ringtom, and more so that he had laid claim to replacing Big Joe. But Ma shook her head and ruined it all. "I'm surprised that there is enough sense in that ugly head to get him out of the rain," she said.

Maybe I'da been better off, I thought, if I had done

a little more thinking about how to deal with women instead of traipsing the hills like Hyford Ringtom. Not thinking of them in the same way as Hyford Ringtom did when he took his fiddle and went to play music for them, but just plain thinking how to coax them into liking a big old ugly dog that nobody wanted.

During the night I got to thinking that the big dog might have sensed Ma's not wanting him on the place. I worried so much about his leaving that I finally got out of bed and sneaked across the floor to where his bed was underneath. I placed my ear to the floor and stopped breathing.

"Big dog," I whispered down, sorry now that I had put so much resin in the cracks, afraid my voice wouldn't reach him.

And the thumping of his tail against the floor was enought to knock the boards loose.

I guess me and that old dog might have parted company the next day if it hadn't been for Pa. The rain had been light and the ground was still dry enough to turn. But the sky above showed signs that it still held barrelfuls, ready to upturn. Pa reckoned that he ought to get his seed potatoes in the ground before the rains made the earth to wet to plow. It would be best, he told Ma, if we waited until the end of the week to take the big dog back. This gave me and the big dog a mighty short time to win Ma's heart . . . a job sure to be bigger than outeating or outbragging Hyford Ringtom.

It was the ugly dog that found the way. During the latter part of the week we were loafing along the slopes above the house when he stumbled on the nest where the chickens were laying wild. Ma had searched for it for the better part of the month. The hens had hid their nest in a clump of wild honeysuckle, and the big dog had just tramped right into the nest. I ran to the house to fetch Ma.

Ma really chuckled as she gathered the eggs in a basket. She filled the empty nest with sharp rocks to discourage the hens from using the hill nest again, hoping to coax them back to the henhouse. Most of the eggs she gathered from the nest would be useless, but she had found the nest, and that was important.

The big dog limped down the path beside her, plain forgetting me or so it seemed. Just walking slow and easy and melting in the praise she was pouring on him. I walked behind, ashamed for the way he was conniving on his own. I'd bet a pretty penny the big dog wouldn't look me straight in the eyes. He knew he had not searched and found the nest with the intentions of Ma taking the eggs to the house. He had stumbled upon it and was intending to keep the eggs. Fact is, he had been sucking one of the eggs when I had come upon him. He was surely an egg sucker, which was almost as bad as running a fox or eating a squirrel after it had been shot from a tree.

Yet, I had mixed feelings about the whole thing. One half of me was shamed all the way to my toes, and the other half was just bubbling over with happiness because the old dog had done what he did. My reasoning was a selfish one: I wanted more than anything to keep the big dog. His acting so frisky around Ma told me that he was counting on me to keep his secret about sucking the egg. I knew now that I could share my secrets with him. We were partners for sure.

I joined the big, ugly dog right then and there. I made show over him. I even lied a little. I thought it was a little, but Pa made my lying as big as a mountain itself. I told Ma that the big dog had killed a copperhead snake that had crawled into the nest to suck the eggs. I got started right off talking too much about the big dog. And that's a habit I have never been able to break.

Ma reached down and patted the big dog on the head. She placed her hands on her hips and grinned. "That old Outcast," she chuckled. And from the look in her eyes I knew that he was here to stay. And she had given him a fitting name—Outcast— even though she had named him on the spur of the moment.

When evening was deep in the hill country and the shadows came out to play over the rugged land, Pa looked at me and said:

"I'm right proud of you, Caleb."

"I reckon I can't rightly claim all the credit, Pa," I says. "The big dog done the most."

"I'd say you done more than your share," he said. "Finding the hens' nest was a fine thing, but to fight off a copperhead until your ma came is a great thing. Yes sir . . . you done something this day that I have never been able to do in all my years here in the hill country."

"What's that, Pa?" I asked, thinking that Pa had about seen and done all there was to do here in the hills.

"See a copperhead snake this early in the spring," he said. "Why, cold weather had not left the hills yet. Every copperhead snake to my way of thinking was holed up somewhere this time of year with the warm earth tucked around him, warding off the cold."

"Well," I said, my face smarting and my neck itching, "it did sure enough look like a snake, Pa."

"I guess them rusty old roots of a honeysuckle can look a terrible lot like the rusty hide of a copperhead," Pa said.

It seemed to me that Pa was aiming to give me a way out. And I was dead set on taking it. Ma didn't know the habits of snakes like Pa did. And I had bragged about it all until the snake had taken on an unusual size. There had been a terrible fight, with the big dog rolling over and over and the snake wrapped around him. And he had fought and killed it just to save the eggs. But I knew now that I wasn't fooling Pa one little bit. I hated mighty bad for him to catch me in a lie. So you can see how happy I was to be given a way out. Well, an old rusty root could look like the hide of a copperhead. Anyone could make a mistake like that.

"Yes, sir, Pa," I said, "it sure did look like a snake."

"Of course," Pa added, "since it was sucking an egg it couldn't of been a vine, now could it?" Pa was grinning, making me squirm now. "But . . . I'd say a dog would be easier to break from sucking eggs than a snake any day of the week, wouldn't you?"

"I sure do hope so, Pa," I said. "I sure do hope so mighty bad."

Chapter Seven

Time seemed to hang silent and unmoving, like a bird nest in the forks of a tree. The days and nights were almost the same. Me and Outcast spent most of our time romping about the hills. We climbed to the tops of all the mountains to look out over the world, and we trailed the ridges and furrowed into the hollows like two ornery groundhogs. It was a sight to see how fast that old dog caught on to all I showed him. To be truthful, there were times that I got to wondering just who was showing who. One minute I would be on my knees pointing out some varmint track and he would be holding back like he was afraid of running into a thorny bush, and then the next minute he would be running the tail right off the varmint.

Up at the rock cliffs, I poked his nose inside the den holes. He always came out snorting and blowing dust about, sneezing like he would turn himself wrong side out. I would double up laughing and the awkward old brute would romp and nuzzle my hands like he was a small pup wanting some attention.

One night he struck the trail and treed an old winter-poor possum. I climbed the tree and pulled the possum out by the tail and ran all the way to the house with it, just like I was holding the biggest and toughest old boar coon in the country. I looked around for a box to keep it in until Hyford Ringtom came over. I wanted him to see what a fine hound-dog I had. But Ma said she did not want an old dead possum on the place, so Pa shucked it out for me and stretched the hide over a board, judging the hide would be enough for Hyford to see. I judged Pa to be right at first. It was a sight to see how big he had been able to stretch out the hide. I made up my story then and there. Never had I seen so mean a possum. I'd tell Hyford that it just wouldn't "play possum." It fought the old dog like a boar coon.

I reckon I had been too excited over catching the possum to stop long enough to judge how well the old dog had handled it. But later I wondered about the old dog's knowledge. I got to thinking that he might be holding back about as much knowledge of the hills as Pa and Hyford Ringtom knew. Maybe he was just pretending, letting a little seep out at a time, seeing how much joy I was getting from thinking I was teaching him. Maybe he was just trying to plow under the miserable years of his past and crowd his whole life into the happy ones left, now that he was with me. Ma said that she had known people of the hills to do just that. They were old people, with their backs bent from time and hard work. They had learned how to sift out the bad years, and had just time enough to live a few good ones before they went to their final sleep here in the hills. Well, it made me happy to think that about Outcast, realizing that I might be giving him powers to think like a human. But what sort of a hound-dog man would I be if I didn't brag a little about him now and then?

Each night after the big dog had crawled under the floor, I lay in bed thinking that Hyford Ringtom was past due to visit. I wondered what he might think about my dog. Old Outcast was far from being a little dog. I loved the big dog and that made up for all his faults and lack of looks. But Hyford would be a stranger to him, and he would not judge him kindly. The big, ugly dog had faults, to be sure. There were the times he shamed me by standing around the kitchen door while Ma was cooking, waiting for her to throw out scraps. Ma often scolded him and said that old Outcast was as much like Hyford Ringtom as a dog could be. There were times that I had to scold him and even get a little mad. But whenever we were out alone I always forgave him his faults and told him so.

And there were times that I knew Outcast was ashamed of me. Like the time he bayed the skunk up at the rock cliff. I just stood below the cliff rolling in joy while his big, mellow voice fought through the brush to reach my ears. For all his ugliness, he had the true voice of a hound, and one long bawl from Outcast was bigger than all the yaps old Rufus ever put together.

At first, I thought that he might have treed a squirrel. I was even a little mad because I hadn't brought a rifle with me. Well, maybe I can't shoot the squirrel out, I thought, but I can just lean back against the cliffs and get my fill of his bawling.

But it wasn't a squirrel at all. He was face to face with a big striped skunk. He kept his distance from it, circling around it to hold it at bay. I felt right proud of him as he limped around in a circle so fast that it made me dizzy to watch. He had guts holding that big skunk like that. Not many dogs would want a skunk. It wouldn't be no time, I thought, until he jumps in and grabs it. He just wants to give me time to see how he can handle it. I'd bet he could grab it and kill it without getting a whiff of scent on him.

I listened to him for a while and then got a little restless waiting for him to go in and get it. I began to resent him looking back at me now and then like he was thinking there was something about this whole thing that I was supposed to do. I was disgusted.

"Get him, Outcast!" I yelled.

The big dog just stared at me in total disgust. I just

did not know that it was his place to hold it at bay and my place to figure out a way to get it out of the circle without either of us getting the scent on us. I got madder at him. I even got to thinking that he was afraid. And then I got mad at the brazen skunk, just standing there in the middle of the circle like he owned the hill country and dared us to take it from him. I picked myself a good-sized club and looked down at old Outcast.

"Just you take note of this," I says to him. "I'll show you how to handle a skunk!"

I started inside the circle and Outcast blocked my path and almost tripped me to boot. He stretched his old body across my path and tried not to let me move an inch closer.

"If you're afraid of that skunk," I said, "get out of my way. You ain't making a coward out of me!"

I blundered on, expecting the skunk to run. He obliged me, but the crazy thing ran straight at me. Then he turned and sighted! I dropped the club to run. There was Outcast, right in my path. We both went down and the skunk's aim was true as a rifle ball. We went wollering down the side of the mountain, sick from skunk juice, vomiting, and gasping for air. And as full as the mountain was of fresh air, we couldn't find a good breath of it.

We went sneaking back to the house like two thieves

about to steal Ma's chickens. My dog stopped at the edge of the woods and would come no farther.

"You can use the rain water in the barrel beside the barn," Ma said. "You first and then Outcast!"

I had intentions of fooling Ma and me and the big dog sneaking into the barrel together. The big dog didn't agree with my thinking. He stood at the edge of the woods with eyes that said I was the cause of it all and that I had a lot to learn. He would trust the rain and weather to take the scent from his coat. And so while the lye soap burned into my hide I told myself that me and Outcast wouldn't be wasting our time again hunting skunks. Their hide wasn't worth much. I figured he'd be agreeable to that. Tomorrow we'd talk it all out good and proper.

Chapter Eight

Me and Outcast had not been together hardly any time to speak of, and yet I could not close my eyes and remember when he had not been on the place. He went with me everywhere—to the well for water and to the woodshed for stovewood. Ma got to grinning and watching how the big dog followed me so close. I got uneasy, figuring she was about to tease. I pretended that I didn't know the dog was so close to me. But if he had strayed a foot away, I would have known it.

For me, the loneliness of the hill country was gone. There was just no way to tell anyone the closeness between me and that old dog. I was so happy I felt like busting at the sides. I reckon Pa knew it though. I guess he had felt the same about Big Joe and the other hounds that he had owned. I knew now how hard it had been for him to bury Big Joe there at the rock cliff and then turn and walk away without him. I didn't think I could leave old Outcast that way. But then, I didn't lay claim to being the man Pa was.

One morning after old Outcast had chased and killed a pesky weasel that had been stealing Ma's eggs, Pa said to me:

"I believe you sure enough skinned old Billy Flint right out of his hide. I tell you when that old Outcast laid claim to Joe's bedding I was concerned. But I reckon now he is dog enough to circle on it any time."

Pa was stingy when it came to praising hound-dogs. Just as tight as Hyford Ringtom was apt to be. A dog had to prove himself. I was proud that Pa had compared Outcast to Big Joe. I had heard him say to Hyford Ringtom that Big Joe had been as good a hound as he had ever owned. And Hyford Ringtom had agreed that Big Joe had been as good as he had seen in the hill country. Of course, Pa had just made a small comparison, but it wouldn't be hard for me to stretch his talk into a mountain of praise.

Each time I thought of Hyford Ringtom I got worried. With a little help from me, Outcast could fool Ma, like he had done over the hens' nest. But Hyford Ringtom would judge him only as a dog. Besides, Hyford would be expecting to see a teeny dog, one like we had talked about that day at his cabin. He would judge Outcast's crippled leg, knowing that it would slow him on a trail. But he would be fair in his judgment. I guess it was only me that was trying to be dishonest.

The possum hide that Pa had stretched over the board had dried out now and had shriveled up until it looked to be the hide of a field mouse to me. I just kept thinking of ways to stretch it back out without it tearing. If Hyford Ringtom didn't come before long, I feared the hide would shrink until it disappeared.

Chapter Nine

Hyford Ringtom came late one evening. It was at suppertime. I came out of the barn to see him standing in the yard talking to Pa. The little feist stood beside him, legs looking like a pair of slingshot forks upside down. Ma had stuck her head out of the kitchen door.

"No, Mrs. Tate," Hyford said, "I didn't come over to eat. Come to see that hound-dog pup that Caleb must have by now. Brought old Rufus over to get acquainted, and to start right off showing that little dog a few tricks. You just can't start a dog learning too young. Been in the hills all day trying to search out poisonweed that one of my neighbor's cows got ahold of."

Hyford had done it this time, I thought, seeing the tiny grin on Ma's face. He had blundered almost as bad as I had done on the copperhead snake. Ma had him dead to rights. The earth was still far too cold for poisonweed to sprout, and Ma knew as much about plants as Hyford did about dogs.

"Why, Mr. Ringtom," Ma said, "how could you expect to find poisonweed when the weather is still too cold for it to sprout?"

Hyford scratched his head and stared toward the sky like he expected the answer to fall from the clouds. He shuffled around.

"When it sprouts it might be too late to search it out," he said. "Got to git it before it sprouts. Dig it up by the roots."

"But how do you know where to dig?" Ma asked, dead set on making Hyford squirm worse than ever.

I reckoned Hyford to be indebted to Outcast right from the start. He just blundered out from under the floor and saved Hyford. My heart was in my mouth. Hyford turned and stared at the big, ugly dog.

"What have we here!" Hyford said, setting back on his heels. He looked at me and then back at old Outcast.

"That's my hound," I said.

Old Rufus ran up to sniff, got too close and the old dog lifted his big paw and knocked the little feist across the yard. He didn't do it out of meanness. That was the trouble. That's what shamed me so. The big dog wanted to play. And everyone knew that a hound-dog ought to be serious, especially Hyford. The only thing that kept me from feeling awful about it was that that little feist came right back to nip at old Outcast's legs

and play with him. This made them both guilty, and Hyford wasn't a man to take merits from his own dog.

"Glory be!" Hyford said. "But this dog has grown considerable from the one we talked about. I'll say this, Old Rufus likes him. That's a good sign."

And then Hyford dropped to his knees to judge him. I almost lost my breath. Hyford knelt there poking his head toward the big dog like a turtle sticking his neck out of his shell. He ran his hands slowly over the coat of the big dog. His face held no expression, good or bad. His hand came to the crippled leg. Here he stopped. He frowned and looked up at me. I guess he could see the hurt in my eyes. He looked around at Pa and then back at me.

"This leg will slow him considerable," he said. He rubbed his chin. "But, you know . . . I'd heap ruther have a slow dog myself. A fast dog stays so close to the feet of the game that a man can't get a shot off. Mighty rugged coat."

"They're the kind that hunt mountain lions out West," I said, hoping to add a few merits to old Outcast.

"Well," Hyford said, "that don't cut much timber here. Old Rufus done run all the mountain lions out of this country long ago."

"Supper is getting cold!" Ma scolded.

"Well," Hyford said, "didn't come to eat. But I just

might take something to drink. It's a job, digging that poisonweed roots."

I stood there mad enough to bite a nail in two. Hyford had said nothing at all for me to feel good about. I didn't know what he thought of my dog.

"Let old Rufus and that big brute get acquainted," Hyford said. "Weather is still cold enough for dogs to run. Come morning, me and you just better take that dog into the hills and try for a mess of squirrel. A yard ain't no place for a man to judge a dog. The hills are the place."

Chapter Ten

The weather did all sorts of things the next morning. March was fighting a last battle with April, and it was a furious fight. April would send the sun streaking through the mountains and the winds of March would try to knock the heat from it before it reached the earth. The footing was brittle and frosty and morning sparkled the tree bark. April was winning out. It had slipped enough sun through the trees to melt frost and patch the earth with dampness.

But it was the wind that favored the big dog the most. Without it, he would have sounded as noisy across the leaves and brush as Muley. The wind was keen on top of the mountain and it whipped the tops of the trees into noises that drowned out the big paws of the old dog. And Rufus, being a mite jealous, wandered off out of sight. Outcast followed.

On the end of a point, old Outcast treed. He just set himself down under a big black gum and bawled loud enough to wake creation. It fooled Hyford to hear such a mellow voice come from such an ugly brute. I could tell by the look on his face.

Well, I'da given a pretty penny if I could have seen a squirrel locked in the forks of that tree. But all we found was old Rufus. He was hitched up a-straddle that big gum farther than I could reach. And it looked to be Rufus the big dog had set his eyes on. Yes, sir, Outcast had gone and treed old Rufus—treed him just like he was a squirrel. But I say this much for him: he did it in the only way he could without embarassing me. I looked at Hyford with pride. He wasn't about to admit that old Outcast could mistake Rufus for a squirrel, and he wasn't about to admit that that little feist had locked his legs around that tree for nothing. Anyone knew that a dog that had chased all the mountain lions out of the country wouldn't climb a tree to get away from an ugly dog like my Outcast. He wasn't going to say that there wasn't a squirrel in that tree, either. If he did, then old Rufus had lied. He was as guilty as my dog, Outcast. So with a peculiar look toward the big dog, Hyford turned to search the black gum tree for a squirrel.

Hyford said that the squirrel was there all right. It was the wind that kept us from finding it. Time was a-wasting, he figured, and we ought to be getting on so that my dog could watch Rufus and learn. Well, Outcast treed Rufus four more times before we reached another point! Hyford frowned at the big dog and said:

"Them two dogs sure do hunt good together." He still judged the wind too strong to see the squirrels. They were crossing out of the tops of the trees, traveling, and when they traveled sometimes it was for miles on end, even crossing rivers. Normally the little feist would have followed them, but Hyford said that Rufus knew the big dog would not be able to keep up.

I was surely proud of Outcast when at last we spotted a squirrel in the top of a tree he was under.

"Shoot him out," Hyford said.

I wiped the wind out of my eyes and toppled him out. I hurried toward where he fell. Rufus wouldn't get him this time.

"Wait!" Hyford grabbed me by the arm. "Let Rufus fetch 'im."

Here goes another squirrel, I thought. Not only that, but the little feist was apt to teach old Outcast some bad habits, like eating squirrel. So it truly pleased me when the little feist brought the squirrel back holding it by the nape of the the neck. Outcast came limping along behind him.

"Now," Hyford said, "we'll teach that big dog to fetch game." He tossed the squirrel over the side of the mountain and yelled fetch. But it was Rufus that brought it back, holding it again by the nape of the neck.

"Once again," Hyford said.

The two dogs were gone for a considerable time. Hyford began to squirm.

"Think I ought to go see about them?" I asked, more worried about Outcast than the squirrel.

"And let them dogs think we don't trust them to bring that squirrel back?" Hyford said. "Give 'em time. I might have rolled that squirrel under a shuck of leaves."

I heard the big dog coming over the rim of the mountain, tramping over the leaves. That shamed me enough. But when he came up over the rim of the mountain holding the little feist by the nape of the neck, I could have died of embarrassment. Rufus was squirming and yipping but Outcast held him fast. He set old Rufus down at my feet, looked up at me like he was wanting praise for what he had done and thumped his long tail against the leaves. Hyford looked down in total disgust.

"That dog has got a lot to learn," he said. "He's lucky old Rufus is good-tempered. He'd be apt to eat another dog up for less than that. Now . . . where is that squirrel? We'd better take a look."

The squirrel was hard to find, being as how there was only about a third of him left. Hyford looked down at the big dog:

"Going to have to break him of eating game!" he

said.

But it was that feist's mouth that was covered with squirrel hairs. And I told Hyford so, not wanting him to take merits from my old dog. Hyford squirmed and scratched his head.

"Just tried to take that squirrel away from that big dog to keep him from eating it," Hyford said. "That Rufus dog will do it every time. Hates to see another dog do wrong."

That day, Hyford Ringtom did not offer his opinion on the worth of the big dog. It was days before he did so. The weather had turned and the sun was hot. We didn't hunt much now. We just loafed the hills. We were sitting on top a mountain watching the world go by when Hyford says to me:

"I never knew old Rufus to take up with another dog. It is a good sign. If that big dog didn't have the makings of a good hunting dog, old Rufus would discard him faster than a squirrel can get up a tree. Yep, you got yourself the makings of a true hound-dog. And with Rufus training him, he ought to make a dandy."

I felt proud now. But I didn't brag. As I looked out over the hill country, I was hoping to goodness that Outcast didn't take after Rufus and go to straddling trees. His legs were crooked enough as they were.

Chapter Eleven

In the hill country, summer is the best time to loaf with a hound-dog. It is the time to sit around and do a little bragging. I learned a lot about bragging that summer but not enough to beat Hyford Ringtom.

Me and Outcast took a few groundhogs to keep Ma happy. When the sun came out, the groundhogs crawled out of their winter dens and dug new shallow ones under the warm earth, close to the top where the sun could seep through to warm them. Mixed with sweet potatoes, groundhogs made a tasty meal. Their hides were good for making shoestrings. All in all, the groundhog was a rich, greasy animal and one of them would stretch a long way around a dinner table, even with Hyford Ringtom's feet sprawled underneath it.

A dog could not do much running during hot weather. Heat brought hydrophobia and staggered dogs out of their senses. Then they went around biting everything they bumped into. Me and Outcast kept under the branches where the trees blocked off the sun. I dug for herb roots and he dug for ground squirrels. Sometimes I scolded him for running too hard. He lowered his head and looked up at me with his sad eyes. But I had to scold him because there was no cure for hydrophobia. I didn't want him to go staggering mad and have to be hunted down and shot.

Most of the running came in the evenings when we went into the hills to bring Muley in for milking. I reckon Muley had crammed about as much hate inside her for the big dog as I had love. Going after her now was just pure joy. She couldn't hide from me. The big dog just sniffed her out and nipped at her legs until she was always glad to go home. I just strutted down the path behind them gloating over how I was getting even with that old cow for all my misery in chasing her— that was before Outcast had come along.

In July the old dog came face to face with death. We had gone into the hills to pick wild blackberries for Ma to make a cobbler. I had worked my way into the center of a big patch and had reached down under a bush to gather a handful of juicy shadeberries. I thought at first the noise to be the scratching of briers across my britches, but I was wrong. Suddenly I was staring a big woods rattler square in the eyes. He was coiled and ready to strike. The only chance I had was to stand perfectly still. But in bending over, a thorny vine had

latched onto the side of my face and it dug in so deep that I felt the blood ooze down the side of my face. The pain became unbearable. And the slow stream of blood itched. I just couldn't keep from moving. And that was all the big rattler was waiting on. I went falling backwards in the brier patch. I lay thinking that I was just about dead, thinking that I would soon feel his fangs in the side of my leg.

The ruckus in the briers caused me to open my eyes even though I thought I was just about dead. Then I saw that it was not a set of fangs on my leg at all but a big brier that had latched onto me when I had fell. I rubbed my eyes and saw Outcast tumbling over and over inside the patch, the snake coiled around him. I knew now that he had been beside me all the time and had grabbed the rattler when it had struck, getting hold of it before it reached me. He shook the snake loose and snapped to get it. And the big snake set its fangs in the end of his nose. He gave a sharp cry of pain, whipped the snake around in a circle and grabbed it in the center. He beat it time and time again against the earth. His hair stood on end and I could hear low, vicious growls come from deep in his throat. He shook it loose from his nose and beat it beyond recognition. Fire had risen into the eyes of the old dog and he fought the snake like it was a mountain lion.

The snake lay silent, except for small quivers as the

sun seeped through to touch what was left of it. Then the old dog limped over, whined, and nuzzled my hand. He lay his ugly head across my lap. I could see blood ooze from his nose. The fangs of the snake were still there. He whimpered again and snuggled close to me as if he thought I was about to leave him or something. Can you imagine that!

The next thing I knew I had the big dog in my arms, running as fast as I could toward the house. By the time I reached the bluff above the house his eyes were closed and he was swollen badly. Luck was with me. Hyford stood in the yard.

I was so scared that all I could say was "Snake!"

Hyford hurried to the low slopes and gathered some cocklebur leaves and made a poultice with them, boiling them over a fire. He pulled the fangs from Outcast's nose and tied the poultice across the small holes.

I just stood looking, not able to say a word. I didn't have to. Hyford knew. Pa reached down to pat me on the shoulder and Ma wrung her hands.

"Time will tell now," Hyford said.

When I was at last able to talk I told what Outcast had done. He had saved my life and now I was willing to trade mine for his.

I felt better when Hyford promised to stay at our house to watch over Outcast. Ma looked down with tender eyes.

"Outcast can stay in your room, Caleb," she said. "With you and Hyford Ringtom. But only until he is on his feet again."

And although she didn't say so, I figured her to be meaning Hyford Ringtom as well as my dog.

The big dog lay silent and swollen for two days. Day and night Hyford changed the poultice. And long after Hyford had gone to bed, I sat with the big dog's head across my lap until daylight came. One morning I fell asleep and Ma caught me there with the big dog's head across my lap. She reached down and patted him on the head.

"He'll be all right, Caleb. For all his trifling ways, Hyford Ringtom knows the right herb cures for hounds," she said. "And it'll take more than a woods rattler to snuff out a great hound-dog like old Outcast." Hyford was so tired from loss of sleep that he did not wake up. So it was Ma who changed the poultice this time. I fell back asleep feeling proud that Ma had at last called him a hound-dog.

Ma was right. The snake bite didn't keep him down for long. Soon he was up and roaming the hills with me for the rest of the summer. Ma bragged over and over again how the big dog had saved my life. It hadn't surprised me. Ma just didn't know how close me and Outcast were. She didn't know that I would have done the same for him.

Chapter Twelve

The snows came early that year and made ghosts of the trees in the hill country. The long, black fingers of trees stuck through the white blanket of earth and the winds quivered among them and made a mournful sound. Hyford Ringtom came with the first snow to see if my work was caught up enough for me to go into the hills with him to track varmints. After the first snow was the best time to catch them. Hill varmints had no worse enemy than a first snow. The snow held every track they made from their den. Ma shamed me by asking Hyford to watch me around the drifts. As if I wasn't man enough to stand beside Hyford as a hunting partner!

Hyford tracked a big red fox to his den up on the side of Tumbleoff Mountain. He was a big, brazen fox mean enough to dig his den right out in the open away from the safety of the rock cliffs, leaving a big, black socket sticking out like a sore thumb along the side of the snow-white mountain.

Since the den was not too far from his cabin, Hyford judged the fox to be the same one that had recently snuck into his yard to steal a chicken. That mean varmint had sneaked inside the henhouse one night and reached up and grabbed what he thought to be a big, fat hen from the roost. But instead of a hen he grabbed old Rufus who was setting there on the roost for just that purpose. Rufus had been waiting on him. Old Rufus tore into him and there was a terrible fight that night. The fight woke Hyford, who had reached the window just in time to see the big red fox going up the side of the mountain with old Rufus on his back. The mountain had gotten so steep that Rufus had fallen off the fox's back, and Hyford had called him back, saving the brazen fox for another time. Now Hyford was ready to settle the score.

"Just you bring that old dog along and we'll show him how to handle a brazen fox that's impudent enough to try to grab a chicken from me," declared Hyford.

The snow was so deep along the mountain that little Rufus burrowed through it like a ground mole, while Outcast leaped up and down in it like he was jumping fences.

The tracks of the big fox led in and out of the den hole. But since it was daylight now, Hyford judged him to be inside. The fox was a night traveler.

"That old fox is a smart one," Hyford said. "There

seems to be only one hole to his den. But old Hyford knows that he's got another entrance to it up there by the roots of that scrub oak."

I followed Hyford to where the smaller hole led out among the roots of the scrub oak. There was less than twenty feet distance between the two holes. Chances were that the two holes ran in a straight line to one another, with a side pocket in between for the old fox to slip in and rest.

"We're going to have to watch this hole," Hyford said. "The knoll between the holes will stop us from watching both at the same time. We'll watch this little hole here among the roots good and proper while I sneak back to the main entrance and fix up the surprise I got for that old fox. I'll fix that old chicken stealer!"

My skin tingled, and not from the cold. I was thinking that Hyford was intending for me to stay here by myself and watch the little hole. Now, I didn't have a bit of use for that old red fox inside that den, and I figured that he had little use for me. And it stood to reason that when two things that had no use for one another met, there was sure to be a fight. I didn't want to tangle with him barehanded. And I didn't aim to fight him like Hyford Ringtom said he had once fought a big fox. Hyford said he had dropped down on his all fours and fought that fox fair and square like a dog. But I could just see that mean fox getting the better of me.

Fact is, if he was as mean as Hyford claimed him to be, I didn't want old Outcast to get ahold of him either. I looked around and found myself a club big as a mountain although it seemed mighty small to me at the time. Mighty small for a fox mean and brazen enough to dig his den right out here on the side of a mountain for the world to look at.

"You won't be needing a club," Hyford said. "We'll just put Rufus here to guard that hole, and you bring Outcast around to the entrance with me so he won't get in old Rufus's way if the fox comes out. You can be sure that Rufus will watch for him. He's still mad that I called him off that fox."

The little feist squatted down and cocked his head to one side like the picture of the dog on a phonograph record back at the house. And I'll tell you seeing that little feist setting there willing to tangle with that brazen fox made me put considerable more stock in him. But I was glad to keep Outcast with me just the same. I didn't see any reason why, if the mean fox should decide to come out the little hole, two dogs ought to get eat up.

Once back at the big hole, Hyford reached inside his coat and pulled out a can of miner's carbide.

"A two-pound can ought to do it," he said. "Ought to just blow him to Kingdom Come."

He stretched his arm back into the hole as far as he

could reach and dug out a pocket of earth with his hand. Then he opened the can of carbide and poured it into the pocket.

"A little water over it now ought to do it," he said. "Ought to fizz it until the fumes get through the hole. We'll throw in a match then and blow that fox out into the open."

"But where will you get the water?" I asked, making a real greenhorn of myself. I was just so excited. And I reckoned old Outcast to be as excited about it all as me.

"The hills are covered with it," Hyford said. "We'll gather some handfuls of snow and fizz that carbide good and proper."

Hyford poured the snow over the carbide. Fumes rose and twirled and drifted as slow as a chicken hawk back through the dark tunnel. The carbide fizzed like eggs frying. A sharp yip came from deep inside the hole.

"Listen to that old varmint!" Hyford said, grinning. "I wasn't completely sure that he was in there until now. We'll give him a good one this time." He raked another handful of snow up and threw it on the carbide, and the frying of the carbide drifted over the stillness of the mountain. Outcast cocked his ears, made a circle around the hole and came back to stand beside me. "You just stand to one side now and keep that big dog out of the way. Watch that brazen fox come stumbling out!"

Hyford scratched a match along the side of his britches. The flames burst from it and he threw it back into the hole. The explosion was enough to deafen you, and the black smoke rolled out of the hole in great puffs.

"There . . . he . . . comes!" Hyford yelled as a black bundle of fur shot past us. It lit on the side of the mountain and rolled downhill, picking up snow as it went, forming a snowball.

I eased down the side of the mountain, trying to hold the big dog back and at the same time trying to keep up with Hyford Ringtom as he chased the snowball. The farther it traveled the bigger it got.

All of a sudden Hyford dived into the air and went sliding down the mountain after the snowball on his belly, using his feet as a rudder to keep him in line with the snowball. He pulled his arms out in a spreadeagle fashion and latched them around the big snowball and went right on riding it down the side of the mountain. Outcast broke from me and went tumbling down the mountain with them.

The big snowball struck the side of a tree and Hyford sat up and straddled it with his legs. He started digging into it with his hands as fast as he could.

I fairly expected to see that big fox poke his head out of that snowball and snip off some of Hyford's fingers. Hyford was growling like a dog as he worked farther inside it. And my dog was working his way

toward them.

Hyford reached the black fur inside the snowball, so black from the blast of the carbide that you couldn't make out what it was. A low growl came out of the snowball and Hyford dug harder.

"Sakes alive!" he yelled. "It's old Rufus!"

He pulled the little dog half way out of the snowball and the little feist was a sorry-looking sight. Stunned from the blast and blinded from the snow, he must have thought that Hyford's hair belonged to that brazen fox that he had sneaked inside the den hole to get. He set his sharp teeth in Hyford's scalp and down the mountain they went again, the feist growling and yipping and Hyford pleading that it was him and not the fox. Outcast, maybe thinking it was the fox instead of Rufus tore into them both. Over and over they went. They reached the bottom of the mountain before the little feist recognized Hyford, and enough of the carbide smoke had washed off the feist for Outcast to sniff and know it was Rufus. Hyford was stretched out, looking like a scarecrow and both dogs were licking his face, when I reached them.

The big fox was a smart one. He hadn't been in the hole at all. He was probably curled up somewhere under a rock cliff, just too smart to stay in an open den with the snow outside to tell on him.

Chapter Thirteen

Now that cold weather was among the hills, a hound could run again. Tom Turner's foxhounds shook the mountains with their deep voices.

I was lying in bed one night thinking about a big boar coon that had strutted through the soft earth not far from Crow Point. I could hear Tom Turner's foxhounds in the distance as they trailed a fox. And I had just begun to think what a useless waste of good dog flesh it was to run a fox, and hoping that old Outcast was under the floor thinking the same thing, when a new voice opened up far ahead of the pack of hounds. I listened closely. I wanted so hard for it to be a strange voice. This hound was far ahead of the pack . . . something that would make Tom Turner furious. It was a bad thing for a hound to break away from the pack and run the fox alone. If he chased too close to the fox, the fox would dive into a hole and the chase would be over.

I cocked my ears toward the window. And the long

bawl of the single hound came again. Then a more shallow voice of a hound opened up beside it. There was no doubt about the shallow voice. It belonged to the speckled gyp, Nellie Bell. I hurried across the floor to where the big dog should be sleeping.

"Outcast," I whispered down. And I waited for the thumping of his tail to answer. Nothing came. Maybe he is asleep, I thought. I whispered again. "Outcast." No thumping came.

A hound-dog man knows the bawl of his own hound. The deep bugle voice came again, so loud this time that it seemed to shake the very hills. I hurried to the window, and there, by the light of the moon, I watched the big ugly dog break into a small clearing above the house. Running a fox! He sniffed the air, looked back, and waited. The speckled gyp broke into the clearing beside him. They romped side by side, sniffing the earth, figuring out the circle that the fox had made here in the clearing to throw them off his track. They worked it out and trailed down the mountain together. I could hear Tom Turner's foxhorn trying hard to call the speckled gyp in.

I stayed at the window until the voices of old Outcast and the speckled gyp died in the hills. I was downcast, looking out over a lonesome stretch of earth. I was shamed by my dog running a fox. I lay across the bed trying to make myself believe it was running the fox that upset me so. But I knew that the hurt was from something else. My big dog was acting like Hyford Ringtom when he spruced up and went fiddling for the womenfolk. I never knew a dog would be like that— not old Outcast. I thought there was only me and the hills, with Hyford Ringtom laced in here and there. But the speckled gyp had slipped in somehow. Funny, I had never stopped to think about old Outcast being a dog and maybe being lonely for other dogs. I thought being with me was enough.

Chapter Fourteen

From that night on, the big dog began to sneak off after I went to bed. I had named Muley a rogue for no more than this. But somehow I could not find it in my heart to call Outcast a rogue.

I kept his activities at nights to myself. I would never let even Hyford Ringtom know that Outcast was sneaking into the hills at nights to coax the speckled gyp from the pack to run beside him. Although there were times during the days that followed that I thought Hyford Ringtom suspected as much. He never said so, that is, right out, but he got to talking about how to break a dog from running fox. He mentioned that there was talk that a strange dog had begun to interfere with Tom Turner's chases at nights. A strange dog that cut ahead of the pack and drove the fox to an early hole. Tom Turner had had him under his rifle sights more than once but the darkness of the hills had marred his aim. The speckled gyp was being lured from the pack by the strange dog, learning his habits. Now, she was next to useless to the other dogs.

"Now," Hyford Ringtom said to me, "if this strange dog was mine I'd tie him up at nights ruther than have him shot dead."

There was a peculiar look in Hyford's eyes as he talked to me. And I knew that Hyford Ringtom was like Pa in some ways—like letting a man work out his own problems.

But I could not tie my dog at night without causing suspicion. Then, for some strange reason, I could not hear him running among the hills any longer. Neither could I hear the speckled gyp. Neither could I hear his tail thumping the boards of the floor as I whispered to him at night. What was he doing?

Finally, I determined to follow him. I let him get far ahead of me but I could still see him in the light of the moon. Up the mountain he went, crossed over and down the other side toward Tom Turner's land. He cleared the fence like a bird and crossed the grazing land. Close to Tom Turner's house he crouched to his belly and crawled toward the dog pens, singling out a single pen a distance from the others. Once at the wire he whimpered low and began slowly to dig at a small hole that showed signs of other digging, fighting to get under the wire and into the pen. The speckled gyp came out of her doghouse, wagged her tail and dug on the other side of the wire. She was in season.

I was afraid to call to him, to let him know that I was there. The other dogs were much too close. The low whimper of a dog would not be apt to bother them, but the strange voice of a human would bring them barking out of the doghouses and light every light in Tom Turner's house. This was where my dog had been coming at nights. He had known she would be here when he had not been able to find her any longer with the pack among the hills.

Outcast worked for the better part of an hour to free the gyp. And with her digging on the other side she finally broke free. Then they trailed off together into the hills.

Outcast did not return home the next day, and it was one of the loneliest days I have ever known. I told Pa that he had probably holed something in the hills and that I ought to go search for him. I had lied to Pa. I left him there to do my work, while I pretended to search the hills to find my dog. I felt bad about lying to Pa. But I felt worse about the old dog choosing the speckled gyp over me, maybe never coming home to make amends for it. Maybe he would remain in the hills with Nellie Bell until they both became wild and had to be hunted down and shot like wild brutes. Hyford Ringtom had known dogs to go wild in the hills and take to killing cattle and sheep.

I spent the better part of the day in the hills just thinking. I reckoned that the big dog loved me all right. And

I tried to think that he was missing me as bad as I was missing him, that he was feeling just as lonely inside and all.

Pa went to town the next day and left me along the slopes mending the fence. I had been working less than an hour when I saw Tom Turner coming down the slopes, and I became very nervous. I thought of all sorts of crazy things as he came closer. Maybe he had shot and killed old Outcast over on his land and wanted me and Pa to pay damage and tote him off. Pa was gone. I would have to handle whatever had happened by myself. Something was wrong. Tom Turner had never visited us out of friendship.

"Lost my speckled gyp two night ago," he said. "Dug under the fence. Ain't seen her about, have you?"

"No sir," I said, feeling a little better now, knowing that he still did not know that Outcast had freed her.

"Well," he said, "there's a reward if she be found." He turned and looked back. "Haven't seen any strange dogs around here lately, have you?" I knew he meant the strange dog that lured the gyp off at nights.

"Nope," I said.

"Got any dogs on your place now?" he asked.

"Nothing but an old outcast," I answered right fast.

I didn't breathe good again until he had disappeared over the rim of the mountain.

The sun had gone down and I had picked up my

water jug to go when from along the mountain slopes I saw a speck moving. I squinted my eyes through the shadows smothering the hills. It was a dog . . . an old dog . . . an old limping dog. I dropped the water jug and ran toward him.

Old Outcast stopped a few feet from me, dropped to his belly and crawled toward me. He knew he had done wrong. He was expecting punishment. His old coat was tangled with cockleburs. I got down, pretending to be picking the cockleburs off, and of a sudden my arms went around the old dog's neck and he just whimpered like he was being whipped.

I didn't have to ask him if he had missed me. The answer was there in his wagging tail and his big, ugly nuzzling head.

I was just so wrapped up in the big dog coming home that I guess I didn't take seriously what Hyford Ringtom said to me a few days later:

"Tom Turner found his speckled gyp. Man brought her to him from down on Johns Creek. Said he caught her with a big crippled part airdale and cur dog. Now, Tom Turner had intended to breed her to a big Walker champion down in Tennessee. He won't be happy about the pup's daddy being an old outcast dog. I'd keep that big dog away from his fence line and out of gunshot. If Outcast crosses the fence, the lasw is on Tom Turner's side."

Chapter Fifteen

I think that me and Outcast might have made it if it had been up to us. We stayed away from Tom Turner's land. The only time we were even near it was in the evenings when we went into the hills to fetch Muley. The grass was tall along the fenceline, browned by weather, with the brown tops doubled underneath as if to dodge the night coldness that painted it white. But picking was poor in the hills and Muley searched out the fenceline for the brown grass.

It was almost dark that evening, when I spotted a break in the fence. I could see where Muley had crossed. Maybe she wanted to find more brown grass and maybe she had gone in search of old Bluetoe. I would never know what went on in that old rogue's mind. Whatever the reason, I knew that I had to get her off Tom Turner's land fast! I could sneak back at daylight and mend the fence, placing brush over the break to keep the sheep in until I could repair it. I only hoped that

Tom Turner did not come by in the meantime.

I tried to make my dog stay on our side of the fence. I knew that Tom Turner often came in the evenings to where the sheep grazed. I didin't want Pa to have to pay to fix the break in the fence. Tom Turner would have him dead to rights if he caught the cow over there. And I remembered Hyford Ringtom's words about the dog, too. Tom Turner would know old Outcast on sight. His crippled leg and old coat would give him away.

I thought about what the big dog was supposed to have done that was wrong. To me, it all seemed right. A thousand and one times, I knew I would give a pretty penny to see the pups when they came and to have one. But Tom Turner would most likely destroy them at birth. That's what men did when their pups were fathered by the wrong dog.

The old cow bawled out not far from the break in the fence. She was on the other side of a humpback knoll, and I could not see her. But I knew from the sound of her voice that something was bad wrong. I hurried over the knoll, the big dog running beside me. In my excitement to get to Muley, I forgot all about Outcast crossing the fenceline.

Muley was backed up against the side of a knoll. And old Bluetoe was off a distance, snorting to make another turn and charge her. I could see blood dripping from her side where he had hit her with his last charge. He charged again. The old cow grunted with the force of the blow and fell to the earth. She raised her head to ward off another charge. But she had no horns to fight with and her neck was weak. All of a sudden, I was sorry that she had been born without horns. She needed them back now. Blood covered the grass and she bawled out again, stretching her neck to follow the next charge from Bluetoe. He hit her hard, rolling her to her side. And she lay helpless now, too awkward to match the strength of the black sheep.

I ran to help her, forgetting all her ornery ways. Muley saw me and lowered her old head and bawled as if she expected me to do something fast. She was trying to tell me with her eyes that she had got herself into an awful mess.

"Hi! hi! hi!" I yelled, picking up a club as I ran toward Bluetoe. I thought he would run . . . I guess I hoped he would. But instead he turned to charge me. I dropped the club and turned to run, caught my foot in a tuft of brown grass and fell. I looked up to see that black mountain of fur charging toward me. I closed my eyes.

The next thing I heard was Outcast's vicious growl. I opened my eyes to see him crouched low, drawing the attention of old Bluetoe. His eyes had turned as red as a winterberry and his rusty coat bristled. Bluetoe turned and charged him. Outcast moved to the side, leaped,

and landed on the back of the sheep; stradding him just like Rufus would a black gum tree. He sank his teeth into the big sheep's neck and rolled him to his back. He quickly loosed his hold and grabbed the sheep by the throat. The big sheep was no match for my dog, Outcast. Bluetoe bleated and I looked to see Tom Turner hurrying up the side of the hill.

I grabbed a hill rock and threw it at Muley. She just stood close by like she was enjoying the fight. "Git!" I said. She hurried toward the break in the fence. I tried then to pry the old dog loose from the black sheep. Tom Turner was closer now. I could hear him yelling at me and the dog.

With a million thoughts going through my mind and each of them saying that I was about to lose my dog, I grabbed the club I had dropped when the sheep had charged me and began to beat old Outcast with it, trying to make him let go of the sheep. He held fast. I beat him unmercifully, until knots raised on his old shaggy coat and a cut came over his eye. I just had to do it. I just had to get him loose! Finally I knocked him loose, and we ran through the break in the fence with Tom Turner close on our heels. The big sheep bleated again and Tom Turner stopped at the fenceline and turned back toward Bluetoe still lying on his back, weak from loss of blood.

"I warned you about running that cow!" Ma

scolded, after me and the old dog had come sneaking into the yard. We had stopped at the edge of the woods long enough to catch our breaths and draw away any suspicion that something was wrong. Muley had come on in ahead of us, her sides bulging from the run down the mountain and the cuts on her making her a sorry sight. "Just look at her!" Ma exclaimed. "That old dog has caused her to fall and nearly kill herself. If that big, ugly dog chases her again he'll be off the place!"

"Yes, Ma," I tried to say in an easy voice. I led Muley into the barn to take what milk she hadn't run out down the mountain. Outcast wanted nothing to do with Ma, so he ran under the house.

I gave old Muley an extra helping of corn that evening and tried to think of just milking her and nothing else. After I had finished, I wiped her sides down and tried to think of what had happened. I was so mixed up I couldn't think clearly. My thoughts were as thick and sightless as the milk in the bucket. Maybe, I thought, I had better sneak out provisions to last awhile and take the big dog up into the hills for a few days. Just until trouble had a chance to blow over like a windstorm. I would leave Pa to handle it all. It would be mean to do Pa this way. But he would understand. He would have done the same thing for Big Joe and the other hounds he had owned.

But when I stepped out of the barn with the bucket

of milk, Tom Turner was standing in the yard. A constable was beside him holding a rifle in the crook of his arm. And Pa was holding the big dog by the nape of his neck. I dropped the bucket of milk. And as I ran toward them I heard Tom Turner say the old dog was a sheep killer. He had attacked his sheep. And I knew how they dealt with sheep-killing dogs here in the hills.

"No, Pa! . . . no, Pa!" I screamed as I ran toward them. "Don't let them do it!"

I didn't have a chance to tell them how the big dog had saved my life when the black sheep had charged me. He broke loose from Pa and ran toward the hills where he could find freedom.

The first shot of the rifle made a thousand and one tiny bells ring in my ears. The big dog stumbled and went down. He crawled to his feet and limped toward the hills. A second shot knocked him down again.

"Over here!" I screamed, running toward him now.

He heard me and turned. Tears blinded my sight and all of a sudden I wasn't thinking about the shots but only about the way I had beat him with the club to break him loose from Bluetoe. I just had to make amends to him for the way I had beat him. I had always made amends whenever I had to correct him for something. He expected it from me.

The big dog dragged himself toward me. But a third shot dropped him before I could reach him. He lay now on his side. I knelt beside him and picked his big, ugly head and placed it in my lap. And then I hugged it and ran my hands through his ragged coat, feeling the welts that I had put there with the club.

"I'm . . . I'm sorry, big dog," I said. And then I buried my face in his fur. And he whimpered; just whimpered like a small pup and went limp in my arms. I looked up at Pa, tears streaming down my face. Tears came from Pa's eyes too, the first I had ever seen there, and he turned and walked into the house.

"You had better go!" Ma said to the two men. "Hurry!" And the two men hurried out of sight.

Pa came out of the house with his rifle in the crook of his arm. He took one look at me and the big dog and turned down the path in the direction the two men had taken.

"Please," Ma said to him. "You will only make things worse!"

Pa stared down the path and slowly turned back toward the house.

"Revenge belongs to the Lord," Ma said.

I picked the big, ugly dog up in my arms, and I carried him to the edge of the woods, where I buried him there under the shelter of a big oak. The big, black sprawling arms of the oak would ward off the hot suns of summer and the cold snows of winter. And I placed a flat rock over the small mound of earth to keep the hill varmints from digging him up.

I sat beside the mound until darkness came into the hills. Ma came. I thought maybe she was going to scold me for staying so long in the hills after dark. Before I had always blamed my lateness on the big dog, saying I just couldn't call him in. It was the same this time. But she didn't scold. She knelt beside the small mound of earth that held my heart and said:

"That old Outcast." Then she burst into tears.

Chapter Sixteen

There is no way to tell how lonely I felt. I guess I just looked at the world as being all bad, with a good streak no broader than a broomstraw. I just went around feeling sorry for myself.

I worked harder than ever, hoping that work might take my thoughts off the big dog. But it was just no use. I dreaded going to bed, afraid I might hear Tom Turner's foxhounds along the side of the mountain, reminding me of old Outcast. Pa didn't have much to say. But one day he caught me away from the house and said: "I am sorta worried over your Ma, Caleb. She is hurt mighty bad over old Outcast. Now me and you know that she is bad to worry. I wish you would try to cheer her up some."

I had never really thought much about anyone being hurt but me. I guessed I was being mighty selfish, and so I tried to cheer Ma up. But I guess I didn't do a very good job. I think she knew that I was just pretending. At times, though, she did seem to feel some better. And at times my talking about it seemed to help me, too. But whenever I went into the hills the hurt came back. I found myself waiting at the top of the knoll for the old crippled dog to catch up. And then there was old Muley. She was up to her same old tricks again. And the big dog was not there to sniff her out of her hiding place. I even got to thinking that she knew that the old dog was no longer there, and she was glad of it. I knew I had no right to accuse her of that.

Worst of all there were times in the evenings when I went to fetch Muley and saw old Bluetoe strutting along the fenceline. I began to accuse him of coming there just to remind me that he had got even with old Outcast for whipping him so. I had less use for him than any creature on earth. And I thought of all kinds of ways to get even—ways that I could get even without causing Pa trouble.

Even Hyford Ringtom and Rufus reminded me of my dog Outcast. But one evening when he came, I got something off my chest that had been worrying me for a long time now. I had just been thinking over and over again how I had beat the big ugly brute and had never had a chance to make amends with him for it.

"How many times do you reckon you had to scold old Outcast?" Hyford Ringtom asked.

"A thousand and one," I answered.

"Did he ever hold a grudge over them?" Hyford asked.

"Shucks no," I said. "He always knew I didn't mean none of what I said to him."

"That's it," Hyford said. "A man and his dog are one. They don't hold grudges against one another. Why, that big dog had forgot all about it before he reached the house. But he sure wouldn't want you to be pouting this way. He'd like to know he had a master that could stand up to anything. That's the way of a great hound-dog."

But the time came when I dreaded to see Hyford and Rufus come over. Both reminded me of old Outcast. Hyford must have sensed it, and he came less often.

Chapter Seventeen

The following spring, the awful storm hit the hill country.

I had gone into the hills to fetch Muley. Clouds had been rolling across the sky for the better part of the day, which was not unusual for March. Yet at times they became so black that they caused Ma to stop and warn me to stay clear of the woods if the wind came up. Inside the woods, trees could fall during the storms and pin you down.

I got to thinking as I walked up the side of the mountain that Ma should have told Muley the same thing when she had wandered off that morning. It would have done little good. She would have chosen the woods anyway. She had to cross through the woods to reach Tom Turner's fenceline and the short tufts of green grass that were trying to sprout along it.

By the time I crossed the top of the mountain, the clouds had come so low that it was already dark among the taller trees of the woods. I had spotted Muley twice close to the fenceline, but both times she had kicked up her heels in orneriness and had gone deeper into the mountains, hugging the fenceline. I chased her for nearly a half mile before she tangled herself in a patch of brush. Dark clouds hovered like the black wings of a crow, flapping apart now and then to allow a touch of light to seep to the earth. I took no chances with that ornery cow. I tied a halter on her and walked her along the fenceline toward home.

I had traveled less than a quarter mile when the winds hit. The tops of the trees touched the earth. First came the rain and next the hailstones. Both knocked me to my knees. I held the end of the rope I had hooked to the halter and Muley pulled to the edge of the woods for cover. She blinked her big eyes as the hailstones beat against her.

It looked as if the whole world would soon be lifted up and carried away like a sycamore ball. The wind scooted me across the earth as far as the end of the rope would allow and the hailstones beat me raw. I handwalked the rope back to the old cow. I pulled myself under her belly, trying to dodge the icy balls.

Muley moved slowly ahead, still close to the fenceline, dragging me with her, until she reached a small cave cut in the side of a rock cliff. We both ducked inside. The winds howled around us as if they were

121

mad because we had beaten them. Above the roar of the winds came the bleat of the sheep across the fence. They were huddled together in a small group. They had no place for shelter. Tom Turner's land offered none. The land had long ago been stripped of trees in favor of grass. And the strong fence kept them from the shelter of our woods. They were just left to the mercy of the storm, a storm that didn't look to be carrying mercy with it, only death and hailstones the size of bird eggs.

Suddenly it became so cold that my fingers grew numb. And my wet clothes soaked up the coldness and froze my body. The heat from the body of the old cow turned the coldness into steam and it rose and almost took my breath. The steam trailed near the edge of the cave and was sucked out by the wind. The bleats from the sheep became wild now. The wind and the hailstones beat them unmercifully.

I guess I didn't mind the hailstones beating against old Bluetoe. That crazy old sheep just kept rounding the others into a tighter circle and holding them there. But I felt sorry for the rest of them. They had done nothing to me. And well, I guess I might as well admit that at times I even felt a little sorry for old Bluetoe. He was just plain ignorant, out there fighting a storm that had whipped him from the start.

And then a queer thing happened. The big black sheep broke and charged the strong fence, picking a small gully where he must have judged the fence to be the weakest. The wind knocked him sideways. He fell, gained his footing and charged on. Just staggered into that fence head on. It sprung him back a few feet, he got up and charged again, hitting it in the same place. He was just plain killing his fool self!

After more than a dozen charges the blocks in the fence began to spread, and one of the strands broke. And each time he charged the fence now he went deeper inside and the sharp edges of the wire cut into his flesh and blood ran over his black hair. He had gone plumb crazy, it looked to me. I got scared. Maybe the old fool had seen me there inside the rocks and was trying to reach me. Maybe he thought that it was me that sicked the big dog on him. If he made it through the fence I wouldn't have a chance to get away. If I tried to climb a tree the wind would blow me out like a winter leaf. I couldn't outrun him, I was so cold and stiff.

The hole in the fence was almost big enough for the old brute to come through. And right then and there the crazy fool stopped. The wind knocked him down and he was slower to get up this time. I guess he had used up his strength, and the loss of blood had weakened him even more.

He staggered toward the flock. He turned them and routed them toward the hole in the fenceline. He crowded them against the fence until one found its way through. The others quickly followed. They went into the woods for cover from the hailstones. Two came inside the cave, squeezing and pinning me against the rock. Muley bawled and kicked. But they chose her kicks to the storm outside. I petted her to keep her from kicking and maybe knocking my head off.

And now old Bluetoe was left in the open field, blood dripping from his face. He staggered in line with the hole in the fence and made a furious charge. I guess he thought he would throw himself through. But the storm had whipped him. He made it halfway and then dropped. The wire held him and the hailstones forced him over on his back and the rains came down like a river through the gully to drown him.

I thought all sorts of things as I sat inside the cave. I thought of the many long nights I had dreamed for just such a sight as this; the old sheep meeting his death, a death just as cruel as Outcast had suffered. And the way he would die now would cause no trouble. There would be no one to blame. Only the storm. And you cannot blame a storm.

"Stay out there and die, you old brute!" I yelled out. "I'm going to sit right here in this cave and watch you die! You got it coming!"

Now, I ask you: Why would a fool sheep beat himself to death by charging into a wire fence? Get himself caught like that and be left to the mercy of the storm that held no mercy? Just to save a bunch of sheep. No, I had to shake this last thought from my mind. To believe that, was to believe that the old brute had a good streak in him. He bleated now from pain and he tried to raise his head but the wire held him fast. And the hailstones beat him terribly.

"Bleat all you like!" I yelled. "There ain't no one to hear you." I couldn't help him, I told myself, even if I wanted to. Why, I couldn't make it to the fence. Even if I did, my fingers were too numb to move the wire.

And this seemed as good an excuse as any. Yes, sir, my fingers were just too numb to move that wire. I tried to move them as I thought about it. Against my body they had suddenly become warm, and I got a little mad when I had no trouble moving them. I wanted a good excuse just in case I got to thinking about helping that old brute. I knew it was wrong to just sit and watch something die.

Now, the harder I tried to quit thinking of that old brute out there suffering, the more I thought of just that. And as I watched him being beat to death a small streak began to appear from nowhere. It was just a small streak of good at first, to be sure. But it grew like a sprout during a warm spring rain. It was a mighty great thing, I began to think, what that old sheep had done. He had saved his flock. He had given his own life to do so. And then for no reason at all I wondered if I would have done the same thing if that had been a field full of people trapped out there. I judged I wouldn't, and I got mad because the old sheep had more guts than me. But he ain't nothing but an old brute, I thought, a helpless brute without power to reason. Just that way because the Lord wanted it so. But he is braver than me and the Lord has given me power to reason. And as I watched Bluetoe die, I felt smaller. I got to talking out loud to myself and the eyes of the big cow crossed mine, like she was wondering what was happening to me. Go right out there and save that old brute and be bigger than he is, something said that to me. Something like Pa's voice. Pa would have said that.

I got to my feet. They felt unsteady and a little numb. The big sheep bleated again. I just couldn't watch him die like this. It had not been him that had crossed the fence in search of trouble.

"Hold on, Bluetoe!" I yelled. "I'm coming!"

The hailstones had turned to rain. This helped some but the wind was still strong enough to blow me to the ground. I grabbed hold of tufts of grass and pulled my way to the fence and pulled myself along to where the sheep lay. And bracing myself I tried to pry the wire loose, but I couldn't. I braced my feet against his side and forced him over on his belly, getting his head out of the water the best I could. But the broken wire had dug into his hide and held him fast. And the cold wind

numbed my fingers. I couldn't break him loose and I knew it. I knew too that he would drown the way he was.

I had only one chance. I dropped to the ground and pulled myself along the earth to the small pine grove close to the fenceline. I pulled my knife from my pocket, blew on my hands to warm them, and cut an armload of pine boughs. I dragged them with me to the fence. And fouling them in the wire I went back for more. After a half-dozen trips this way I brought some long splints from a wind-broken tree. Bracing myself against the fence, I built a lean-to over the old brute. I wove the pine boughs in and out, lacing a fair shelter from the rain.

I felt weak now. So weak that I could not stand against the wind or pull myself back to the cliff. I crawled back inside the lean-to and ripped a piece of cloth from my shirt and wiped the blood from the old sheep's eyes. I could see the helplessness in them. But as I stared into them things began to turn around on me. I staggered and almost fell to my knees. I was numb and dizzy. I would rest awhile, I thought, and then everything would be all right. The wind and rain would slack off before long. The wind was dying now. The rain would soon follow and then I would get Muley from the cave and take her home. I crawled up beside the old sheep to gather what warmness came from his body. The smell of the wet, black hair was rank but it was only warmness I wanted, or cared about. I heard the dying patter of the rain against the pine boughs.

I don't rightly know how long I lay there like that. I was too weak and sick now to care. I remember seeing two lights. They flickered across the open land and I judged them to be stars. I thought that the storm must have ended, since stars will not come out to play across the sky until a rain is gone. The stars looked awful close to earth. And then the earth and sky began to meet, so close now I thought the sky would slap me in the face. Suddenly the stars became lanterns and two men stood over me and the black sheep.

"Help me get him out." The voice belonged to Pa.

Then Tom Turner took off his coat and placed it around me. I couldn't imagine Tom Turner doing such a thing. Giving me his coat and standing there in the cold and rain in a thin shirt.

Chapter Eighteen

I cannot account for the next few days. I was out of my head with fever. I was saying all sorts of crazy things. But when I finally did open my eyes and got my bearings, I saw Ma and Pa and Hyford Ringtom all three setting there on the edge of my bed.

It was Hyford Ringtom that smiled and said that my fever broke and that I would be all right, as long as the fever did not take a notion to come back. And if it did, he had the herbs to fight it again. He raised my head and made me drink a glass of herb juice. And then they laughed and talked about all the crazy things I had said, shaming me something awful. Crazy things like calling out to old Bluetoe. Can you imagine! Seems that I had been worried the past few days, thinking that he was still hooked there in that fence without a soul to help him. Pa grinned as Hyford talked. My face smarted, because I knew he was thinking that I had found a broad streak of good in that mean old sheep.

Pa finished by saying that the old sheep was going to be all right. And then he shamed me right good and proper in front of Hyford Ringtom by saying how proud he was of what I had done. He didn't know of the many times I had told Hyford Ringtom how I was going to handle that old sheep when the right time came around. I tried to think of a reason for saving him. Something I could say right fast to ward off what Pa had said. I couldn't think of a thing. I did try hard to belittle what I had done, giving credit to the old sheep for saving his flock. But the more I talked the more Pa swelled his chest and shamed me.

Next Pa told of the bad things I had said to my old friend Hyford Ringtom, and I felt just awful about them. On the third day I had opened my eyes and seemed to be better. Then I started crying out for the old, ugly dog, Outcast. Right then and there Hyford had offered me his little dog, Rufus. This was the greatest thing that Hyford Ringtom could have done, since he was as close to Rufus as I had been to old Outcast.

"I wouldn't have that little tree-straddling varmint!" I had said to Hyford Ringtom.

Pa said that tears welled up in his eyes and he went out on the porch to sit a spell. Hyford had been sitting up day and night watching over me. He had slept on the hard floor beside my bed rather than take a soft bed Ma had fixed for him in another room. I just didn't know what to say to him now to try to make amends. But I reckon Hyford knew how bad I was squirming. And he got me out of it:

"That old Rufus ain't much to look at," he said. "I guess it is just this old heart of mine that he fills."

"He's the best squirrel dog in the hill country!" I said, defending him there in front of them all.

Then they told me how old Muley had remained low on the slopes for the first time since we had owned her. It had been her milk, along with the herbs, that had strengthened me. And Tom Turner had come to see me every day since I had been sick!

But the thing that hurt me the worst of all was Pa saying that now Hyford had a job working for Tom Turner. I looked at Hyford as Pa talked. I felt sick all over again. Especially when Hyford says to me:

"Going to spend my days in the hills now searching for snakes . . . the sort of snakes that are apt to sneak up and snatch them little foxes. Shame the way them snakes is thinning them little red foxes out. When Tom Turner asked if I could handle this job myself, I said if I can't, I know where I can get a partner, soon as he's well." Hyford Ringtom looked at me and winked.

I drew up my mouth like I'd just bit into a green apple. "I ain't aiming to work for Tom Turner," I said.

"Shame," Hyford Ringtom said. "He took down all them posted signs from his place, so a man can cross over to hunt and be welcomed. Be hard to do by myself, I reckon. Well, he says to me, you going over to John Tate's place? Reckon so, I says, I been in the hills gathering herbs for Caleb."

"Mind taking this pup of Nellie Bell's over to Caleb?" he says. "Man that hunts on my place has got to have something to hunt with, I figure. Only had the one, she did, and it's pure airedale. I'm a foxhound man myself."

Hyford pulled the pup from his hunting coat. He sat it there on the bed, and it got in bad trouble right off by chewing on Ma's blanket that she had spent the whole winter making. Ma stomped her foot and the pup scurried up into my arms. All of a sudden I was holding the spittin' image of my old dog. Ma placed her hands on her hips.

"Just a little outcast," she chuckled.

I tried to think of something fast to say, something to add merits to my dog. Hyford saw me squirming. He got me out of it.

"Them's the sort that hunt mountain lions out West," he said.

Pa grinned. And I had the uneasy feeling that he was thinking I had found a good streak in Tom Turner. Pa was almost always right.

About the Author
Billy C. Clark

A discussion of Billy Clark (1928-   ) may aptly begin with *A Long Row to Hoe* (1960), a narrative of reminiscences and perhaps Clark's best and most warmly received volume. His seventh published book and the story of his life through high school, it makes clear that the wellspring of his career was his background growing up in a semiliterate, impoverished home on the Big Sandy River near Catlettsburg. The volume tells of a ragged family living at the junction of the Big Sandy and Ohio: an intelligent father, a shoemaker and a fiddle player, whose literacy was limited to signing his name and who told his son about poor people "having a hard row to hoe"; the mother, a laundress who played the piano and was so generous of heart, according to her husband, "She'd give away a chair with someone sitting in it"; and eight children. One of Clark's greatest regrets has always been that his parents were unable to read his books.[1]

"In nineteen years of growing up in the valley, hunger was my most vivid memory and an education my greatest desire," Clark declares as he tells of how as a boy he trapped for muskrats, set trotlines, salvaged flotsam, and scrounged for whatever small sums of money he could get. It is not psychological scars, however, that Clark writes about but the learning and the lore that came from the rivers, the community, and the people who were a part of his growing up. In fact the *Time* review of *A Long Row to Hoe* (July 25, 1960) concluded that Clark, "far from trying to forget his boyhood miseries...has dignified them through grit and awareness of the natural beauty around him." And the *San Francisco Chronicle* reviewer (Oct. 2, 1960) observed that Clark's reader "comes to the end of his book envious of his opportunity to have had such a wonderful childhood."

After graduating from high school--the point at which *A Long Row to Hoe* ends--Clark spent four years in military service during the Korean War and then entered the University of Kentucky in 1953. He tried to pay his way with the help of the GI Bill, carry on his studies, and do the writing that had been a compulsion even during high school days. Clark says that when he was enrolled in a writing class, "Hollis [Summers] recommended that I drop his class" on the grounds that, "You are the first natural-born writer I've ever met, and your writing is changing in class." But Clark insisted on completing the course, and as his works make evident, he managed to preserve his own way of looking at things and the distinctive characteristics of style and manner that in another writer might be called defects.

During his years as a college student Clark managed to publish *A Heap of Hills* (1957), a collection of stories, and to get ready for a burst of publication--five volumes during the next five years. One was *Song of the River* (1957), a novel he had written when he was a freshman in high school. It is the story of an aging man who lives in a shantyboat on the Big Sandy and whose aim in life is to catch a legendary great catfish known as Scrapiron Jack. The main thread of the story is reminiscent of Hemingway's *The Old Man and the Sea*, but what makes the novel distinctly Clark's own is his detailed portrayal of the life on the river.

In *The Trail of the Hunter's Horn* (1957) a boy, Jeb, has worked long and hard to earn a pup of his uncle's wonderful hound, Lucy, and is bitterly disappointed when the pup turns out to be stub-tailed and blind in one eye. As the novel progresses, however, and in its sequel, *Mooneyed Hound* (1959), love between the boy and the dog replaces all other considerations, the animal shows prowess as a coon dog, and Jeb enters him in the annual trails for the best coon dog in Kentucky. Reviewers noted two qualities in these novels that make them something more than just juvenile stories about a boy and a pet. One is the author's sensitivity in developing the relationship between the boy and his dog; the other is his responsiveness to the rugged beauty of the land. "This book," says the *Saturday Review* of the first volume (Oct.19, 1957), "has a quality of universality which makes it one of those stories which haunts the reader, no matter what his age. It is evident that Mr. Clark loves the hills and rivers and the people about which he writes."

Riverboy was published in 1958 and was followed by *A Long Row to Hoe* and then by three more volumes that are characteristic of Clark at his best: *Goodbye, Kate* (1964), a story of a vagrant mule that becomes a community nuisance; *The Champion of Sourwood* (1966), which tells of an agreement whereby thirteen-year-old Aram Tate agrees to teach a wily woodsman, moonshiner, and cockfighter to read and write if the latter will get Aram a hound dog and teach him about "the varmints and the mountains"; and *Sourwood Tales* (1968), a collection of eighteen stories that picture life in the Big Sandy region during the Great Depression. In all these works Clark's sometimes extravagant yarns hold his stories together, but nothing perhaps equals the author's portrayal of the local life and lore and his responsiveness to the surrounding natural beauty. The sounds of rustic music, the roughhewn and unsophisticated mountain and river characters, and the humor and pathos in human and life situations--these make Clark the chronicler of the Big Sandy region.

William S. Ward

*Titles in **bold type** are in print and available from the Jesse Stuart Foundation.

[1]Quoted from William S. Ward, *A Literary History of Kentucky* (Knoxville: The University of Tennessee Press, 1988), 353-355.

The Jesse Stuart Foundation

Incorporated in 1979 for public, charitable, and educational purposes, the Jesse Stuart Foundation is devoted to preserving both Jesse Stuart's literary legacy and W-Hollow, the eastern Kentucky valley which became a part of America's literary landscape as a result of Stuart's writings. The Foundation, which controls rights to Stuart's published and unpublished literary works, is currently reprinting many of his best out-of-print books, along with other books which focus on Kentucky and Southern Appalachia.

Our primary purpose is to publish books which supplement the educational system, at all levels. We have now produced more than fifty editions and have hundreds of other regional books in stock, because we want to make these materials accessible to students, teachers, librarians, and general readers. We also promote Stuart's legacy through video tapes, dramas, and presentations for school and civic groups.

Stuart taught and lectured extensively. His teaching experience ranged from the one-room school-houses of his youth in eastern Kentucky to the American University in Cairo, Egypt, and embraced years of service as school superintendent, high-school teacher and high-school principal. "First, last, and always," said Jesse Stuart, "I am a teacher...Good teaching is forever and the teacher is immortal."

In keeping with Stuart's's devotion to teaching, the Jesse Stuart Foundation is working hard to publish materials that will be appropriate for school use. For example, the Foundation has reprinted eight of Stuart's junior books (for grades 3-7), and a Teacher's Guide to assist with their classroom use. The Foundation has also published many books that would be appropriate for grades 6-12, including Stuart's *Hie to the Hunter*, Thomas D. Clark's *Simon Kenton, Kentucky Scout*, and Billy C. Clark's *A Long Row to Hoe*. Other recent JSF publications range from college history texts to books for adult literacy students.

James M.Gifford
Executive Director